Henry Reed's
Baby-Sitting Service

Henry Reed's Baby-Sitting Service

by Keith Robertson

Illustrated by Robert McCloskey

A YEARLING BOOK

Published by
Dell Publishing Co., Inc.
1 Dag Hammarskjold Plaza
New York, New York 10017

For information address The Viking Press, Inc.,
New York, New York.
Yearling ® TM 913705, Dell Publishing Co., Inc.
ISBN: 0-440-43565-X
This edition published by arrangement with The Viking Press, Inc.
Printed in the United States of America
Fifth Dell Printing—May 1979
MPC

To Hope Hexter who has put the finishing touches to many a manuscript

Henry Reed's
Baby-Sitting Service

Sunday, July llth

Well, here I am back in Grover's Corner, New Jersey.
I've been here less than two days, but I feel right at home.
Aunt Mabel looks the same; Uncle Al looks and acts the
same; and my beagle Agony almost went crazy, he was so
glad to see me. It's been about ten months and I thought
he'd forget me, but he didn't. I don't think elephants have
a thing on beagles when it comes to remembering.

This is my second summer in Grover's Corner. My father is in the diplomatic service and I've lived most of my
life abroad. My Aunt Mabel and Uncle Al invited me to
spend last summer here in Grover's Corner so I could see
what the United States was like. I'm glad they invited me
back again this summer because I like it here. I flew in to
San Francisco and then drove across the country with the
Glasses. They're neighbors here, and they have a daughter

9

named Midge who is a year or so younger than I am. There wasn't anyone else even close to my age in Grover's Corner, so Midge and I became good friends. In fact we went into a research business together and made almost forty dollars each.

The Corner hasn't changed much since last year. There is one new house, which makes a total of ten. The Cassidys have moved away and so have the Marples. Two new families have taken their places, but I understand their children are all babies; at least they are all too young to go to school. The family in the new house has little tots too. The big change, however, is that the Apples are gone and Siegfried, their cat, went with them. Mr. Apple was very peculiar and grouchy. Mrs. Apple was always complaining—particularly about her cat. And Siegfried, the cat, was just plain mean. They didn't have any children, or if they did they were grown and gone and were probably mean too. A family by the name of Sebastian bought the Apple house and has been living there about six months. According to Aunt Mabel there are twins in the Sebastian family, a boy and a girl a little older than I am.

My mother owns four acres in Grover's Corner near Uncle Al's house. At one time my grandparents' house was there, but it burned down years ago. Now there's nothing left but an old barn, some empty lawn, and several acres of trees. Midge and I used the barn for our research business last summer. This morning I decided to go look things over. Also, since the lot is next door to what is now the Sebastian house, I thought I might bump into the twins. My beagle Agony and I were up on the second floor looking at the pigeons that live there, when I heard someone downstairs.

"Hi!" Midge's voice shouted. "How's everything look?"

"Pretty much the same," I said, coming downstairs. "You said that a new family had moved into the Apple house. You didn't mention that they had a couple of kids."

"Hardly worth mentioning," Midge said noncommittally.

"What do you mean?"

"They go away to school, so I haven't seen much of them. Besides they're a lot older than we are. They're seventeen."

The way Midge talks you would think she was the same age as I am, but of course she isn't.

"That's only two years older than me," I said. "And I might remind you that you're a year younger than I am and I manage to stand you."

"The year between us makes only a tiny difference," Midge said, unwrapping a piece of gum and putting it into her mouth. "The two years between you and the Sebastian twins makes a big difference."

"Why?" I asked. "I'm very mature for my age."

"I know you are," Midge said. "You're too grown up to chew gum for instance, which is why I didn't offer you any. But the Sebastian twins have drivers' licenses, which makes them so much older than we are that we don't exist."

I knew what she meant. Getting a driver's license makes lots of teenagers think the world has stopped turning just to look at them. But sometimes they want to show off by driving younger teenagers around. I suggested it might be handy to be on good terms with the Sebastians.

"Don't waste your time. Take my word for it, they're impossible."

"Aside from thinking a driver's license is so important, what's wrong with them?"

"They have a few small faults," Midge said. "They're stuck up, rude, conceited, selfish, uninteresting, overbearing, loud, and dumb."

By this time I suspected that Midge didn't like the Sebastians. "They can't be that bad," I said.

"It isn't easy, but they manage," Midge said. "I've got a theory that houses and people and cars all affect one another. The Apples built that house, and it got a nasty, disagreeable disposition from them. Then the Sebastians bought it and now they're that way too."

"And you think the house made them that way?" I asked. It was an interesting idea—sort of silly but fun to think about, like ghosts.

"That's right. Ruth and Johnny Sebastian have a little red MG. It may not belong to them but they seem to have its use for the summer. That car has a nasty disposition."

"A car can't have a nasty disposition," I said.

"Yes, it can. All of its own. Just you wait and see. That car actually does mean things all by itself. And of course it's just the kind of car that would go with the house."

"That doesn't make much sense."

"Yes, it does. Like attracts like. Now, I'm attracted by a house that's charming, gay, and graceful."

"And has bats in the attic," I added. That kept her quiet for a minute. In fact she made a face at me and changed the subject.

"Are we going to run our research company again this summer?" Midge asked.

We walked outside and looked up at the sign on the end of the barn that said "Reed & Glass, Inc., Pure and Applied Research." I had painted the sign myself, and it was a pretty good job. However, it looked faded, and I couldn't work up much enthusiasm about going back into the research business. Besides, as my uncle Al says, there are almost as many research firms around Princeton as there are beards. The field is getting badly cluttered with amateurs.

"I don't know," I said. "It takes so long to build up a reputation that the summer will be almost over by the time we get rolling."

"That's right." Midge said. "We started earlier last year. Maybe I'll start a dancing class. That would look nice up

on the end of the barn. 'Mademoiselle Glass's School of the Ballet.' You can be my stage manager."

"*You* teach dancing?" I asked. I guess I sounded as though I didn't believe she knew anything about ballet, which I didn't.

"Yes, me," Midge said, putting her nose in the air. Since the end of her nose turns up anyway, when she puts it in the air she *really* looks offended.

"When did you learn ballet?"

"I'm starting Monday. In fact I'm going to see about my schedule in a few minutes."

"If you are just beginning yourself, how can you teach?"

"I'll stay one lesson ahead of my pupils," Midge said. "That way everything will be fresh in my mind. I have a math teacher in school who I'm sure teaches the new math that way. If he gets two lessons ahead he gets as mixed up as we are."

"I think the whole idea is silly," I told her. "There aren't any little girls in Grover's Corner the right age to take ballet. And no mother is going to drive her child out from Princeton to take lessons from a girl who is just starting."

"Why don't you think of a better idea?" Midge asked in an annoyed voice.

It had been raining during the night and was starting to drizzle again, so instead of standing there getting soaked I decided to do just that—go home and think of a better idea.

"I'll give the matter some consideration," I said, and called Agony to go home. "It shouldn't be difficult to come up with something better than a ballet school. I can just see you and your pupils clomping around like a bunch of fat, clumsy chickens."

Of course if there is anything that Midge isn't, it's either fat or clumsy. Girls never have any sense of humor though about being either, and Midge just looked at me, tight-lipped, without answering. It began raining harder, and I started home. I was next to a puddle of water when suddenly a car seemed to come out of nowhere. There was a flash of red and then a sheet of muddy water drenched me from the waist down. Agony was almost washed into the ditch. I stood there dripping and sputtering while Agony gave a yelp and scuttled for home.

"If you had studied ballet you could have leaped gracefully out of the way," Midge said. "You just met Ruth Sebastian."

"Why didn't you tell me that car was coming?"

"I didn't see it. That proves what I said. That little MG is a sneaky, nasty car. It pulls little tricks like that."

Of course Midge is ridiculous. Cars don't have dispositions any more than houses do.

Monday, July 12th

It rained most of yesterday afternoon, last night, and this morning. I've spent a good part of the time reading. I'm lucky that Aunt Mabel and Uncle Al have books in the house. Uncle Al is interested in sailing ships and has a number of books about early American ships and captains. I didn't know until last night that I have ancestors who went to sea. Uncle Al told me all about them.

"You mean your mother has never told you about the seafaring Harrises?" he asked. "One of your ancestors was the skipper of a ship in the China trade out of Marblehead, Massachusetts, and another member of the Harris family built ships. My grandfather told me we had a whaler in the family too, but I've never pinned down just who he was. You come from a long line of seagoing Harrises. There's practically salt water flowing in our veins."

17

"That's odd," Aunt Mabel said. "I've never been able to get you to spend even a week at the beach. And the only time you ever went deep-sea fishing you got terribly seasick."

"That's because we Harrises like real deep water," Uncle Al said. "And that sand on the beach gets between my toes and I'm uncomfortable."

I read several of Uncle Al's books. The Harrises back in eighteen hundred and all the other seagoing colonists were certainly men. They could do anything, and they weren't afraid to try anything. Boys went to sea when they were twelve. Some of them were captains of ships while they were still in their teens. One man had a ship when he was eighteen, sailed around the world by the time he was twenty-two, and had made a fortune and re-tired by the time he was twenty-six. It's fun but discouraging to read about people like that. Here I am fifteen, and I'm not even started on a career, much less a fortune. I pointed this out to Uncle Al.

"Well, it was easier in those days," he said. "I wouldn't feel too discouraged."

"I don't see how it was easier," I objected. "One man even had his ship attacked by Indians when he went into a port in Oregon. There were all sorts of storms, and the ships weren't half as well equipped as they are today."

"True, but the red man was no obstacle compared to

red tape today. If I had to choose between fighting Indians and filling out all the papers you need for clearance, I'd take the Indians. I'm afraid you better stick to your schooling and not run off to sea. You're going to need the education."

"I wasn't planning on running off to sea," I said. "But I would like to do something this summer to earn some money. If I wait until I get through school and college to start on a fortune, I'll be as old as some of the sea captains were when they retired."

"Well, I don't think they really retired at those early ages," Uncle Al said. "They just moved ashore, set up as merchant traders, and spent the rest of their lives eating too much and telling tall tales about how adventurous they were when they were young. However, I think it's a very commendable idea for you to earn some money. The trouble is that the employment opportunities in Grover's Corner are somewhat limited."

"I'd rather start my own business than have a job," I told him. "I'd like to do something that takes some initiative and judgment. Something with some danger in it."

"That's a rather tall order for Grover's Corner," Uncle Al said. "We don't have any wild horses to be broken and there isn't much prospecting in New Jersey's mountains. Why don't you continue your research organization long enough to learn what sort of business would succeed best around here? You could make a survey and ask all the neighbors what they need. Then you'd know if you could expect any customers before you start."

That sounded sensible, although, as Uncle Al said, you can't think of any of our neighbors wanting anything very adventurous done.

"Do it properly," Uncle Al advised. "You draw up a questionnaire and I'll have it mimeographed at the office. Then you take it around and interview people. Tabulate the result and you'll have a good indication of what kind of business will succeed."

I've been working on the questionnaire for several hours now and I've about run out of ideas. It's going to be something like this:

GROVER'S CORNER SURVEY
Conducted by Reed & Glass, Incorporated

1. Would you like your lawn mowed regularly by a dependable person?
   ——Yes ——No
2. If the answer to the above question is "yes," would you prefer to have him supply his own mower or use your own? (If the mower is furnished the cost will be 50¢ more per hour.)
   ——Supply own mower ——Use my mower

3. Would you like your garden weeded regularly?
——Yes ——No

4. Do you have a swimming pool?
——Yes ——No

5. If the answer to question four is "yes," would you like a lifeguard & swimming instructor for your children?
——Yes ——No

6. If you have horses, would you like them exercised regularly?
——Yes ——No

7. Do you have any trees you would like chopped down and cut into fireplace wood?
——Yes ——No

8. If you have a boat, would you like a competent young man to help keep it in shape and to assist in sailing it?
——Yes ——No

9. Do you have any small building you would like painted?
——Yes ——No

10. Would you like your car washed regularly?
——Yes ——No If yes, how often?————————

11. If there are any other services you would like, kindly indicate below.

———————————————————————————

When Uncle Al gets home I'll show him my questionnaire. I hope he likes it better than Midge did. She took one look at it and was annoyed. Women are peculiar.

"The questions are all slanted," she said. "That's the worst thing you can do with a poll."

"What do you mean, they're slanted?"

"They're slanted toward men. What could I do in that list except act as lifeguard?"

"You could wash a car, ride a horse, or weed a garden," I pointed out.

"I don't know how to ride, I hate weeding gardens, and besides if I start weeding other people's gardens, Mom will make me weed ours. As for washing cars, I'm too short to wash the top."

I tried to point out to Midge that the questionnaire wasn't based on what she might do, but on what people might want done.

"Who's most important, you or the customer?" I asked.

"I am," she said, with her nose in the air. "If you expect me to do most of those things on that questionnaire, I'm retiring from the firm of Reed & Glass, Inc. I suppose I get a pension."

"You do not. The firm's money was all divided last fall."

I could see there wasn't any point in arguing with her, so I came home and put the final touches on my survey form.

Wednesday, July 14th

Uncle Al brought one hundred mimeographed copies of my questionnaire home last night. I've spent the entire day on my survey. I interviewed every family in Grover's Corner except our own house, the Glasses, and the Sebastians. I figured the first two weren't necessary and no one was home at the Sebastians. After lunch I got on my bike and got most of the houses within two miles. I had the people fill out the questionnaire, fold it, and stuff it through a slot in a paper-box.

Most of the people I interviewed were women because the men were away at work. I did find a few men who were retired or home on vacation. Still, about three out of four were women, which may account for the results I got. I didn't have the votes all counted until almost nine o'clock.

"How did you make out?" Uncle Al asked, coming over and standing behind my chair.

"Not very well," I said, pointing to the pad of paper where I had added the score for each of my questions.

"Well, well, well," Uncle Al said. "Now that's what I'd call a fair cross section of public opinion and attitudes in the Grover's Corner–Princeton area. Any good pollster will tell you that the results have to be interpreted by a brilliant expert like himself before you can arrive at the true meaning."

"What do you think these mean?"

"Well, I don't consider myself an expert, but I'm honest," Uncle Al said. "Let's take them question by question. Not many people want their lawns mowed. Since you say most of the people you saw were women, I'm not too surprised at that. Most wives figure their husbands don't get enough exercise anyhow, so they can convince themselves they are looking after their hubbies' welfare and saving money at the same time. Very few people want their gardens weeded because most of them are too lazy to have vegetable gardens. There are more flower gardens, but flower gardeners are usually particular and they figure you wouldn't know a flower from a weed."

"How about the swimming-pool results?" I asked. "Eight people have pools but they don't want a lifeguard."

"That's not surprising," Uncle Al said. "After they've put in the pool they can't afford a lifeguard."

24

"I guess I didn't ask the right questions," I said, very discouraged.

"Let me see your tally sheet and the questionnaires," Uncle Al said. He took them back to his chair and studied them for a few minutes.

"I think you got some fairly conclusive results," he said. "There are only two families around here that have horses. Neither one is worried about having them exercised, but I see you got one request for labor to clean the stalls regularly. You didn't get any bites on the boat question although several people around here have boats."

"I can explain that," Aunt Mabel said. "They want to do their own work. A man who won't lift his hand around the house thinks it's fun to work all day cleaning and polishing his boat. Just why, I've never understood."

"I see you got several tentative jobs washing cars," Uncle Al observed. He paused for a minute to read the remaining questionnaires.

"Well, there's no question whatever about what's wanted," Uncle Al said. "Eleven people say there is a desperate need for baby-sitters."

"A lot of good that does me."

"What's wrong with that? There's nothing here that says anything about what sex of baby-sitter is wanted."

"A boy be a baby-sitter?" I asked.

"Boys often baby-sit," Aunt Mabel said. "You've been living abroad and aren't aware of what has been going on in America. Baby-sitting is the great teen-age employment opportunity and lots of boys are taking advantage of it. Some women I know prefer boys."

"Well, I'm not going to baby-sit," I said. "That's a sissy job."

"It all depends on the attitude," Uncle Al said. "Be a he-man if you want to and go chop wood all day for seventy-five cents or a dollar an hour. Or sit in a comfortable chair and watch TV while some three-year-old sleeps."

There was something to what he said, but there are a lot of drawbacks to baby-sitting too.

"I don't want to have to change diapers," I said finally. "I don't know how."

"Don't take care of tiny babies," Aunt Mabel suggested. "Baby-sitting is a very responsible job. Much more responsible, for example, than exercising someone's horse."

"It may be a responsible job but it's uninteresting. Nothing ever happens."

"That's the mark of a good baby-sitter," Aunt Mabel said. "Nothing should ever happen."

"Most things in life are ninety per cent boredom," Uncle Al said. "You've been reading stories about the early sailing days. They're full of adventure, but the parts about all the long, dull days of light winds have been omitted."

The idea of baby-sitting still seems pretty dull no matter what Aunt Mabel and Uncle Al say, but there don't appear to be any other good business opportunities. I can

26

save the money I earn and spend it on something exciting like a trip to New York.

"I could form a company and call it 'Henry Reed's Household Helper Service,'" I said. "Then I could do anything around the house from baby-sitting to washing windows."

"I'm against it," Uncle Al said. "It sounds too imposing. I'm thinking of starting a one-man crusade against high-falutin names. Undertakers are now morticians, janitors call themselves custodians, and I read the other day where the garbage collectors of one city threatened to strike unless they were called 'removal engineers.' If you are going to be a baby-sitter, be one and be proud of it. Advertise yourself as the best, most efficient, levelheaded, resourceful baby-sitter in central New Jersey. People always respect a man who takes pride in his job and does it well."

I guess Uncle Al is right. I'll be a plain old baby-sitter. It's going to be dull, just sitting around watching people's kids, but then I guess being a banker and sitting around watching people's money would be even more uninteresting. I'm going to put out an announcement. I've got it all drawn up and Uncle Al has promised to have it mimeographed.

HENRY REED'S BABY-SITTING SERVICE

A new business has been formed to serve the greater Grover's Corner area—HENRY REED'S BABY-SITTING SERVICE.

27

Henry Reed, a dependable, resourceful, competent young man will take excellent care of your children weekdays and Saturdays during daylight hours, or evenings until midnight. Special late hours can be arranged.

Standard rates are $1.00 per hour. Lower rates can be arranged for contracts covering a number of days, or the entire season.

Don't entrust the children you love to just *anyone!* They deserve *the best.* Call HENRY REED at HA 9-1234.

Satisfaction Guaranteed

Friday, July 16th

Uncle Al had my announcement mimeographed and brought home a whole bundle of them last night. I distributed about twenty-five, and this morning, right after breakfast, I got my first job at the Wittenbergs. I was a little worried, but I need not have been. There isn't much to being a good baby-sitter. I have a bump on the back of my head, two skinned knees, and my stomach is sort of queasy, but otherwise everything went fine. In fact, the same woman had me come back later this afternoon. What's more, she said that I was not only resourceful and competent, but that I was very discreet too. I wish I'd thought of that word. I'd have used it in my announcement.

I'm fairly certain that Midge is going to join the firm. She was a big help today; I earned two dollars and fifty

cents in the morning and four dollars in the afternoon.
Midge earned two dollars, and Mrs. Wittenberg gave both
Midge and me a dollar tip. Baby-sitting must be expensive
if people go out much. Uncle Al says the high cost of baby-
sitters is the only thing that keeps the highways from
being clogged with cars bumper to bumper.

I arrived at the Wittenbergs at ten-fifteen; I'd never met

any of the family before. Mrs. Wittenberg is a tall, pleasant, dark-haired woman about thirty. She said she had asked about me and had had very good reports.

"This is Danny," she said, introducing her four-year-old son. Mrs. Wittenberg wasn't looking at him at the moment, so Danny stuck out his tongue at me. It didn't seem to be a good beginning.

"I'm chairman of the hospital fund drive and we have a meeting at ten-thirty. I should be back by twelve-fifteen or twelve-thirty," she explained as we walked toward the car. "So there's really nothing to do. I'll get lunch for Danny when I get back. I know you two will get along splendidly."

A big black poodle came bouncing up and sat down beside me. He wagged his entire hind end, he was so friendly. I like poodles. They're almost as nice as beagles. I'd thought of bringing Agony, but decided against it. It was just as well, since the poodle might not have been so friendly toward another dog.

"This is Consommé," Mrs. Wittenberg said. "He's very well behaved and he knows enough to stay off the road."

She didn't say anything about Danny's being well-behaved and I soon figured out that she had a good reason not to. The minute her car was out of sight, Danny grabbed a little wagon that was sitting by the garage, jumped in it, and went rolling down the macadam drive toward the road. The drive has quite a slope, and the way he was gathering speed, I figured he would roll right out to the middle of the street. While the road through Grover's Corner isn't any turnpike, quite a few cars use it. I could see my baby-sitting career coming to a fast end if anything happened to Danny. I ran like mad and managed to catch him before he got to the road.

"You don't want to go out in the road, Danny," I told him.

"Yes, I do," he answered.

"The cars will run over you," I warned.

"I'll run over them," he said. "I'll knock them right in the ditch."

Danny sure had self-confidence. I wasn't so confident, though, so I pulled him back up the sloping driveway to the garage.

"Why do you call your dog Consommé?" I asked, to change the subject.

"Cause he shakes like jellied consommé when he wags his tail," Danny said. "He's afraid to go out into the road, the 'scairdy-cat!"

"Let's go inside," I suggested, and started walking up the drive toward the side door of the house. I figured it would be safer inside until I got used to him.

He didn't say anything, and a second later I heard the wagon behind me. I turned around and he steered straight for me. He skinned both my shins but I kept my temper.

"That's the end of that," I said, when I could walk again. "You can't use the wagon if you're going to go out into the road."

I took the wagon inside the garage and found a nail on the wall. I lifted the wagon up and hung it beyond Danny's reach. Then I took him by the hand and we went inside.

"I don't like you," he said, glaring at me.

I could have told him my opinion of him, but managed not to. Aunt Mabel warned me that the main thing I would need to be a good baby-sitter was the patience of a saint, but I hadn't figured on needing it so soon.

"I want some disinfectant to put on my legs where you ran into me," I told him.

"I'll show you," he said, and led me upstairs to the bathroom. He climbed up and opened the medicine cabinet and without hesitating took a bottle off one of the shelves. "That's what Mom uses when I cut myself."

I glanced at the bottle and saw that it was a disinfectant and not hair oil. I found a piece of cotton and dabbed some on my shin, and then I almost jumped through the window. My mother had used iodine on me dozens of times, but it didn't begin to sting the way this stuff did.

"Stings, doesn't it?" Danny asked.

"It certainly does," I said, wondering what would happen if I strangled him. "Worst stuff I've ever used."

"That's what I tell Mom," he said seriously. "She says I make a big fuss so I wanted to see if someone big like you said it stings."

I felt almost sympathetic for a few minutes. He did have a point. The stinging began to go away and he invited me into his room to see his toys. He certainly had a roomful. We got along well enough for almost ten minutes. Then he opened one of his windows, unhooked the screen, and leaned out.

"Watch this airplane go," he said, throwing out a little balsa-wood airplane. "Hey, look at it swoop! Whee!"

"Look out, Danny, you'll fall out that window!" I said.

He didn't pay any attention but leaned out farther. I grabbed his arm and pulled him back inside.

"I didn't see where it went!" he screamed. "You made me lose my airplane!"

"I'll find it," I said. I leaned out the window myself and looked around. I couldn't see the airplane anywhere, and I was about to give up when a noise made me wonder what Danny was doing. I started to pull my head back in and didn't quite make it. Danny was closing the window. I'll never know if he was hoping to trap me so I couldn't get back inside, or whether he really wanted to slam it on my head. Anyhow he succeeded. It caught me on the back of the head and almost knocked me silly. I sank back on the floor of the room with everything going around in black circles.

When my head finally cleared enough to see, all I could focus on was Danny grinning from ear to ear. I forgot about having the patience of a saint. I reached out and grabbed him by the arm. I pulled him over and flopped him over my knee. Then I gave him two healthy swats on the seat of his pants.

He got to his feet and looked at me very solemnly. "That hurt," he said.

"I expected it would," I told him. "It probably didn't hurt half as much as that window did on my head. Just remember I'm bigger than you are, and I can hit harder than you can."

"I think you're meaner too," he said.

"I specialize in being mean," I said, without smiling.

"All right, I'll be good," he said.

He meant what he said. We had no more trouble the rest of the morning. We went outside and played ball. We were having a good time when Mrs. Wittenberg got home about twenty minutes after twelve. She paid me two dollars and a half, and Danny actually seemed sorry to see me go. I went home and worked most of the afternoon on a model airplane that has a small engine and actually flies. About four-thirty the telephone rang. It was Mrs. Wittenberg.

"Henry, could you come over and baby-sit for about an hour? An emergency has come up."

"Sure," I said. "I'll be there in ten minutes."

35

Danny met me at the kitchen door. Mrs. Wittenberg came hurrying down from upstairs a minute later, fastening on her earrings.

"It was awfully nice of you to come on such short notice," she said. "I'm in sort of a jam. John's boss and his wife have been in Boston visiting their daughter and are on their way back to Cleveland. They just called from New York. There wasn't much else I could do but invite them for dinner and overnight."

She got out her mirror and put on some lipstick. "It isn't like it sounds. They're both very nice, and I'm delighted to have them. It's just that this is unexpected and I'm not prepared for guests for dinner. Naturally I'd like to make a good impression. It's hopeless for me to try to give them directions to here from the turnpike, and even if I could it was Mrs. Bartlett calling and she wouldn't get them straight. So I said I would meet them at the Hightstown exit."

"Can I go along?" Danny asked.

"I think you'd better stay here and help Henry. What I need most, Henry, is to get things organized. I've been trying for ten minutes to get my husband, but the telephone is busy. And I have to go because if they make good time, we'll both get to Hightstown at about the same time." She handed me a slip of paper. "Here's Mr. Wittenberg's number. He's usually there until about five-thirty. Keep calling until you get him. Tell him the Bartletts are

36

coming for dinner and the night, and he's to pick up a nice big steak and we'll cook it on the grill. Also some tomatoes for the salad. Luckily I baked an apple pie this afternoon."

I took the piece of paper and wrote down *Bartlett, Steak,* and *Tomatoes.* Mrs. Wittenberg was all flustered about her husband's boss coming to visit, but I was calm and efficient just like my advertisement said.

"John mowed all the lawn except that part to the right of the path there in the back yard," she said, pointing out the kitchen window. "Of course that's just the part that needs mowing if we're going to eat outside. Danny will show you where the mower is. Would you mow that and see that everything around the grill is neat? Then, if you have time, would you lay a charcoal fire? By that time John ought to be home."

"I'm to have the fire ready for lighting, but not to light it?" I asked.

"That's right. I'll leave everything in your hands. I know I can depend on you, Henry."

As soon as she drove off I went inside and tried to call her husband's office. It was busy the first two times I called, but finally a woman answered the telephone.

"Mr. Wittenberg is not in," she said. "He had to go out on an important call and he won't be back this afternoon."

"This is Henry Reed of Henry Reed's Baby-Sitting Service," I told her. "I'm calling for Mrs. Wittenberg and it's very important that I get in touch with him. Is there some place I can call him?"

"I'm afraid there isn't. He asked me to call Mrs. Wittenberg and say that he wouldn't be home until six-thirty or a quarter to seven."

I went outside and mowed the little patch of lawn while I thought about this. Mrs. Wittenberg was going to get home before he did, and when she found nothing had been done and there was nothing to cook, she'd be really upset. She was nervous about the whole visit anyhow. I laid the charcoal fire and tidied up around the grill, and then I went inside and called Midge.

"I ought to do something because all the stores will be closed before she gets home," I said after I had explained the situation.

"We've got a couple of packages of potato puffs in the freezer," Midge said. "We could lend her those. Also I'm sure we have tomatoes. But we don't have any steaks. The only thing we've got is a beautiful roast of beef and I'd be shot if I took that."

"Could you bring the potatoes and tomatoes over?" I asked. "I'll see if I can find anything here."

I looked through the refrigerator. There was half a loin of pork, the remains of a piece of corned beef, and some luncheon meat. There was lots of cheese, some dishes with some odds and ends of vegetables, and three bottles of milk. Finally, on the bottom shelf, I found a plastic bag

38

with some uncooked chopped meat. The freezer compartment had an assortment of vegetables and a half gallon of ice cream.

Midge arrived on her bicycle a minute later. "Midge Glass's Emergency Food Service coming to the rescue of the natives!" she called from the driveway.

After I had introduced her to Danny, I told her about the food situation.

"Well, the guests eat hamburgers, I guess," Midge said. "Potato puffs, salad, hamburgers, another vegetable, and apple pie with ice cream. Not bad at all."

"I like hamburgers," Danny said. "I want two."

"We haven't any rolls," Midge said. "And I know we haven't any at home."

Aunt Mabel usually keeps several packages in the freezer, so I called her. We were in luck. Midge stayed with Danny while I rode home for the rolls. By the time I got back it was a quarter to six. Mrs. Wittenberg should have been back from Hightstown, but there was no sign of her.

"She could have missed them or they might have been held up by traffic," I said.

"Well, let's get everything ready," Midge said. "We can make the salad and put it in the icebox, and get the hamburgers ready. I know how to make a wonderful barbecue sauce if she has catsup, soy sauce, and mustard."

Cooking isn't too difficult. The three of us had fun. It

got to be six-thirty and still there was no sign of either of the Wittenbergs. By this time the salad was made, the potatoes were in the pan in the oven, ready to be turned on, the rolls were ready to be heated, and we had a pot with a little bit of water all ready for the string beans. The hamburgers were made and on a tray covered with waxed paper, and Midge's special barbecue sauce was mixed and waiting in a dish. I went out and lighted the fire.

Mrs. Wittenberg arrived at ten minutes to seven. The Bartletts had got off the turnpike one exit too soon and had waited for her for fifteen minutes before they learned their mistake. I was standing by the barbecue when the two cars came in the driveway. Mrs. Wittenberg looked at the lawn I'd mowed and the outdoor table which was all set, and smiled happily.

"Everything looks lovely, Henry. Is Mr. Wittenberg inside?"

"He's not home yet," I said. "He left word that he'd be home about a quarter to seven."

Mrs. Wittenberg looked rather sick. "Then he didn't get my message?"

"No, he had left the office before you left here. Midge Glass is in the kitchen though. She's my partner. We borrowed a few items from her house and we have things about ready. You'll have to eat hamburgers, though, instead of steak."

40

"I love hamburgers," Mr. Bartlett said, coming over to look at the fire. "Fire looks about right."

Midge brought out the platter of hamburgers and Mr. Bartlett helped me cook them. In fact he did most of the cooking. Midge had made an extra big pot of her barbecue sauce, and each time Mr. Bartlett turned the hamburgers, he put on more sauce. They were beginning to smell good when Mr. Wittenberg drove in. He barely had time to wash his hands before everything was ready to serve. Midge brought out the potatoes and beans and rolls from the kitchen, and Danny carried out the big bowl of salad. It was a smooth well-organized operation and a delicious-looking dinner.

Mrs. Wittenberg asked us to stay, which we had expected. By this time it was a little late for either of us to get anything at home. We had plenty of everything, so we set up a card table for Midge, Danny, and me. Consommé, the poodle, went back and forth between tables and got titbits from everyone.

Everyone seemed to enjoy the food, especially Mr. Bartlett. He came back twice for hamburgers. "I'll have to get your recipe for that barbecue sauce, young lady," he said to Midge. "Best hamburgers I ever ate."

There wasn't much cleaning up to do except to throw the paper plates and trash in the incinerator. Midge and I cleaned up our table and were ready to go while all the

adults at the other table were still eating their pie and drinking their coffee. Mrs. Wittenberg walked down the drive with us.

"I can't tell you how much I appreciate your pitching in like this. Instead of being in an embarrassing situation, I

think we've made a very good impression on John's boss."

She paid us and said, "I also owe you some food. I'd better write it down so I'll remember."

"Two packages of potato puffs, four tomatoes, and two packages of hamburger rolls," Midge said.

"What about the hamburger?"

"That was yours," I told her. "I found it in your refrigerator."

Mrs. Wittenberg looked very peculiar. "In a plastic bag?" she asked.

"That's right. On the bottom shelf."

"That was Consommé's ground horse meat," she said, swallowing twice.

Midge began to giggle. "Mr. Bartlett wanted my recipe. Wait till he hears it!"

Mrs. Wittenberg managed a smile. She reached in her purse and handed us both a dollar. "I'm not trying to bribe you, but I'd appreciate it if you'd not say a thing about this to anyone—and especially not until the Bartletts have gone."

"You can trust us," Midge said. "Wild horses couldn't drag a word from us."

Mrs. Wittenberg gave a feeble smile and hurried back to her guests. Midge and I rode off on our bikes. I got to thinking about those horseburgers and wondering what the horse had looked like. My stomach began to churn a little.

"Do you feel a little queasy?" I asked Midge.

"Never felt better," Midge said. "I'm a real chef. Anyone who can take old horse meat and make it into delicious hamburgers so that the guest of honor comes back for seconds and thirds, is a culinary genius."

44

I'd had seconds, which didn't make me feel any better. "Don't you feel peculiar, eating horse meat?" I asked.

"Yes, it makes me want to kick up my heels, except I can't because I'm riding a bicycle."

Midge is a good friend and you can depend on her in an emergency, but she can be childish at times. That horse meat didn't bother her a bit. Women are supposed to be more sensitive than men, but I doubt it.

Midge and I were about half the way home when suddenly a red MG swooped by us. About ten feet ahead of us was a fresh patch of macadam or whatever the black tarry gravel is called that they use to patch holes in blacktop roads. The rear wheels of the MG hit that just as the driver gave it an extra spurt of gas. They kicked up tiny black tar-coated gravel and sprayed us. I was in the lead and about four pieces hit me in the face. They really stung. A few also hit my shirt and blue jeans, but that didn't bother me. I was about to say something when I heard a scream of outrage from Midge.

"Look at my white blouse," she said.

I stopped to look. Her white shirt was now a salt-and-pepper shirt in front.

"That's tar—it won't come out," she said. "That will cost more than I made baby-sitting. They did that deliberately! I told you they were stinkers!"

"Who is?"

"The Sebastians! When you see that red MG it means

45

trouble. How they're able to think up so many nasty tricks, I don't know."

"They couldn't have planned that," I pointed out. "We had to be pedaling down the road at just the right spot; the road had to be freshly fixed; and they had to come along at exactly the right second."

"They could have been hiding and waiting for the right moment," Midge said.

"Hiding where?"

"They're so low they could hide behind a little flat rock," Midge said. "And that mean little car helps them pull their dirty tricks. Weren't you splashed the other day?"

Of course Midge is being silly, but this *is* the second time that MG has splattered me.

Sunday, July 18th

There's been a slight recession in the baby-sitting business. I lost a big contract covering two days of baby-sitting a week. The worst part is that the girl who got the job is Ruth Sebastian. She is real sneaky competition, and I have to give some thought to a countercampaign.

I met both Ruth and Johnny Sebastian yesterday. I suppose a newspaper would say I met them "socially," only I wasn't very social before the evening was over. The food was good but the company was awful. At least the Sebastian part was.

Midge appeared yesterday morning looking very annoyed and said, "I'm having a cook-out this evening and you're invited."

"What are you having to eat?" I asked.

"It isn't very polite to ask what you're having to eat

when you're invited out to dinner," Midge said, very haughtily. "I'm having food."

"I just want to be certain I'm not going to eat horse meat," I explained.

"No horse meat," Midge said. She didn't smile. In fact she looked put out at having to invite me.

"I'll come," I said, "even if you don't sound very enthusiastic about the whole idea."

"I'm not," she admitted. "And you won't be either when you meet the others who are coming. Just remember you've agreed to come and it's very rude to back out later."

"All right, who else is coming?"

"Ruth and Johnny Sebastian," Midge said in a disgusted voice. "I wonder how old parents have to be before they learn that it's impossible to pick their children's friends. Mom's got the idea that if we four just get to know each other, we could have loads of fun together this summer. So she is forcing me to have a cook-out for them, which I don't want to do. Their mother is probably forcing them to come, which they don't want to do. We'll all sit around and hate each other and have indigestion."

"There's going to be just four of us?"

"No, Debbie and Ginny Fowler are coming from Princeton and are bringing their cousin Chuck from Philadelphia. I take ballet with Debbie. The Fowler girls are fun; Chuck is shy but all right."

"Maybe it won't be so bad," I said hopefully.

"Don't be an optimist. I couldn't stand it," Midge said, glaring at me. "Would you like to come over and help me get things ready about five o'clock?"

"Sure!" I said, since she had come to my help the day before.

"I'm afraid that you'll have to eat hamburgers again," Midge said. "That's what Mom got."

"I didn't have hamburgers last night," I reminded her. "This will be a pleasant change."

An hour or so later I was mowing the front lawn on Uncle Al's riding tractor when a blue sedan pulled up beside the road. There was a nice-looking woman driving. She slid over to the side next to the lawn and rolled down the window. I drove up beside her and turned off the motor.

"Are you Henry Reed?" she asked.

"Yes, ma'am," I said, looking very serious and dignified.

One nice thing about the baby-sitting business is that it's easy to spot possible customers. A little girl, about five, looked out of the back window at me. She was a funny-looking little thing with big eyes that looked bigger because of thick glasses, and very straight black hair that hung down below her ears. She had a peculiar way of staring without blinking or wavering that made me uncomfortable.

"I'm Mrs. Osborn," the woman said. "I live up near the

next corner in the red brick house on the right. About a mile from here."

"I know the place, Mrs. Osborn," I told her.

"I've halfway agreed to help a friend by taking care of her gift shop for two days a week for the next few weeks. Mondays and Tuesdays from ten to six. I'll know tomorrow evening. Would you be free those two days, say until the middle of August?"

"Let's see, Mondays and Tuesdays," I said, pretending to think. "I believe both days are free."

"What would your special contract rate be for two days a week for at least three weeks?" she asked. "I could be home a few minutes after six, so you would be there eight hours a day."

"For that volume of business our rate drops to seventy-five cents an hour," I said. "That would be six dollars for an eight-hour day."

"*Our* rate?" Mrs. Osborn asked.

"I have an assistant, Miss Margaret Glass," I said. "She's a very competent young lady."

"I see," Mrs. Osborn said. "Well, I should know definitely by tomorrow night. I'll give you a call then."

"Fine," I said. "I'll hold Monday and Tuesday open until then."

She drove off and I went back to mowing the lawn. Baby-sitting at the Osborns' was my idea of a deluxe assignment. I would be certain of twelve dollars a week, and it happens that the Osborns have a beautiful swimming pool in their back yard. I drove into their place once with Aunt Mabel when she was collecting for some charity, and I had a good look at the pool. I could picture myself lounging beside the pool and earning seventy-five cents an hour at the same time.

I was still feeling good about the idea when I went to Midge's at five. Mr. and Mrs. Glass were going to a neighbor's for dinner so we set the table for the seven of us on the screened-in back porch. I told Midge about the job prospect.

"Sounds interesting," Midge said. "Maybe I'll substitute for you if you get tired of swimming or want to go someplace."

"I suppose I'll have to get some lunch for the little girl, but she looks like the kind that eats peanut butter and jelly sandwiches, so that shouldn't be too much trouble."

"What's wrong with peanut butter and jelly sandwiches?" Midge asked.

"Nothing except that they're unfit for human consumption," I said.

"I love them!" Midge announced.

Of course I should have expected that. Girls tend to like peanut butter and jelly sandwiches and boys don't. Girls don't like to go fishing either. It would help a lot if there was a boy about my age near Grover's Corner. This was why I was halfway looking forward to meeting John Sebastian. In spite of what Midge said, he might not be too awful.

We had the table all set and I had the fire ready to light when the guests began to arrive. The Fowler girls seemed nice enough. One was sixteen and the other fourteen, but they were the same size and looked so much alike I wouldn't have been able to tell which was which except for the braces on Ginny's teeth. The cousin, Chuck Wagner, was all right but he wasn't interested in anything except baseball and food. We got along fairly well and were just beginning to be friendly when the Sebastians arrived.

After fifteen minutes of the Sebastians, I was ready to agree with Midge. I gave up any ideas of becoming pals with Johnny.

First, I'd better explain what the Sebastians looked like. They didn't look like twins, for one thing, or even like brother and sister. The only way they resembled each other was that they were both obnoxious. I disliked them on sight.

Ruth was a tall, skinny girl with a horse face. She had a long nose, which she kept in the air as though she smelled something very disagreeable. Her long stringy black hair flopped around her face and she wore black horn-rimmed spectacles. Her clothes looked as though she had forgotten to take out the coat hangers, and they weren't the right kind of clothes in the first place. She had what my father calls "that grimy-dingy intellectual look." He says there are a lot of long-haired characters who seem to think brains and being clean don't go together. I don't mean Ruth was dirty—just sloppy.

Johnny was taller than his sister but pudgy. He had a crew cut and was well scrubbed, but looked no more attractive than Ruth. He sat around without saying much. Most of the time he looked sullen, but now and then he'd stir himself to make an announcement and to look superior. He may not have cared much for the company, but he appreciated the food. The way he and Chuck Wagner ate, I wasn't certain anyone else would get anything to eat.

I felt sorry for Midge. In less than fifteen minutes Ruth Sebastian had managed to scare the Fowler girls so that they were afraid to say anything. Whatever they said, she corrected them or managed to make them appear like little kids. She was clever the way she did it. Ginny Fowler said something about looking forward to spending two weeks at Beach Haven. Ruth smiled as though she were about to reach over and pat Ginny on the head and said, "I used to be wild about the shore when I was younger, but now that I have my driver's license and can run down any time I want, I think that more than a day at the beach is sort of a bore."

After a few remarks like that, she practically had the floor to herself. She liked to talk, and we sat there listening to all the wonderful places she had been and how im-

portant she and her family were. Finally, about the middle of the meal, Midge asked me to help her get more Cokes for everyone.

"If that Sebastian girl says just once more, 'Way back when I was young before I got my driver's license,' I'm going to rub a hamburger in her hair," Midge said when we

got in the kitchen. "Henry, you've got to do something!"

"*I've* got to do something?"

"You're the only one who has traveled a lot and met people she hasn't," Midge said. "She hasn't mentioned going to Europe. Tell some stories about being in England and meeting the king."

"There isn't any king," I told her. "England has a queen."

"All right, tell her about how you met the queen."

"But I didn't meet the queen."

"Don't quibble about details," Midge said. "Do you suppose she's sticking to facts?"

"Well, I'll try to think of something," I said. Nothing seemed to come to me at the moment. Some people have the idea that if you live abroad life must be very exciting. The most exciting time I ever had was last summer, right here in Grover's Corner.

"And don't tell her how come you've traveled so much!" Midge warned.

We took the Cokes back to the table just in time to hear Ruth Sebastian say, "I studied ballet once. We were spending the summer in Maine and a ballet master from Paris happened to be there, and he had a special class. Remember that summer, Johnny?"

"Uh," said Johnny. That was all he ever said when she asked him a question. I wasn't sure whether it meant yes or no. Maybe he had his mouth so full of food that he couldn't make any other sound.

"It was loads of fun but it seems childish now. I think ballet is wonderful when a real professional performs, but it's sort of silly for amateurs."

I halfway agreed with Ruth, but my father is in the diplomatic service and I would have known better than to make such a remark with two ballet students around. I sat back waiting for the explosion.

Debbie Fowler just looked hurt, but Midge was boiling. Midge's hand tightened around the Coke bottle and I figured that was one bottle we would lose our deposit on. Then she remembered she was the hostess.

"Henry, tell Ruth about the girl in Naples you knew who became a ballet star," Midge said.

"I didn't know any girl in Naples who took ballet," I said.

Midge took a deep breath and glared at me. I was willing to cooperate but it takes a second or two to think of a good lie. Then I remembered a tightrope artist who used to live next door to us. There was a son who was about my age, and the father used to tell us two boys stories about his adventures. I imagine he stretched the truth, so changing his stories even further wouldn't hurt much.

"I think you're talking about a woman we knew in Rome. She had studied ballet as a girl. During World War II she was put in a concentration camp. She was on the second floor of a building and she managed to walk across a pipe to the top of a wall. It was only because of her training in ballet that she was able to do it. Another woman behind her lost her balance, fell, and was killed."

"That's right, it was Rome," Midge said with her nose in

the air. "It was an opera singer you knew in Naples, wasn't it?"

This set Ruth back for almost five minutes. Then she began boasting about being at the Mardi gras in New Orleans. She talked about this about twice as long as necessary. Finally Midge got a chance to break in.

"That sounds very much like the festival in—where was that, Henry?"

"Seville," I said. "Actually it's a Holy Week, but it's a carnival too, the biggest in Europe. The ambassador to Spain went to it and he invited us as his guests."

Midge grinned happily. "What foreign countries have you been in?" she asked. "Any besides England, France, Spain, and Italy?"

"Switzerland, Holland, Belgium, Germany, Portugal, Austria, Ireland, Greece, Turkey, Israel, Egypt, India, Australia, New Zealand, Japan, and the Philippines," I said.

"That's right, you had just been around the world when we met you in San Francisco," Midge said. "You know, I feel hungry again. I think I'll have another hamburger."

Ruth Sebastian was speechless. She looked at me wide-eyed and I felt sort of mean. After all, the only reason I'd been to so many places is that my dad's job takes us there. It can get tiresome traveling so much, and going to school gets confusing. I haven't spent more than one year in one school since I was six.

58

"What are you doing here in Grover's Corner?" Ruth asked.

"Baby-sitting," I said.

"Baby-sitting?" Ruth asked, looking at me as though I were crazy.

"Well, with all Henry's experience he really should call himself a tutor," Midge explained. I could see she thought mentioning baby-sitting took away from my glamour as a world traveler.

"Henry and I have formed a baby-sitting firm," Midge said. "After all, he speaks French fluently, and I can teach ballet. You know, if we take that Osborn job, you ought to teach the little Osborn girl some French."

"Is that the Osborns who live up near the corner?" Ruth asked.

"That's right. The place with the swimming pool," I told her. "She wants someone Mondays and Tuesdays."

The Sebastians left shortly after that. Ruth had been squelched and Johnny had stuffed himself so that he couldn't eat any more.

Although the Sebastians lived about half a block from Midge, naturally they had driven over in their red MG. It had been parked in the driveway annoying Midge during the entire meal. Ruth drove over and Johnny drove back. He got in the car, raced the motor several times, and then went roaring out of the driveway. There was a watering can sitting near the driveway part of the way down so he made a big swerve to the opposite side and ran over about six feet of plants near the edge of the black-top drive.

"Great!" Midge said. "Those are some fancy ruffled petunias that Mother started early. She'll blow her top! Now you see what I mean about that car?"

"Car nothing, that was Johnny's bad driving."

"Oh, he did it deliberately," Midge said. "But somehow that nasty little car knew those were special flowers."

"I like MGs," Debbie Fowler objected.

"It isn't MGs in general, it's that particular one that Midge dislikes," I explained.

"I'm not going to hold my breath until they invite me to their house," Midge said. "But I hope they do, so I can refuse. All in all it's been a successful evening. Henry, you saved my life. She was boiling!"

I didn't know how boiling mad she was until noon today. I got a call from Mrs. Osborn.

"Henry, you needn't hold Mondays and Tuesdays for me. I happened to meet a girl at church today who was looking for a job those particular two days."

"Yes, ma'am," I said. I couldn't think of anything else.

"You probably know her, Ruth Sebastian. She wanted to do some practice tutoring because she's planning to become a teacher. In fact she's had some courses in kindergarten work, and being with Belinda will be helpful to her. Anyhow, thank you very much."

"You're welcome," I said. "Just in case you should change your mind or Ruth Sebastian should get sick, the firm of Reed and Glass is always at your service."

I saw Midge during the afternoon. When I told her what had happened she was furious. Suddenly she was a full-fledged member of the firm and she felt she'd been robbed.

"That mean, underhanded rat fink! This is war! Henry, getting even is a matter of honor now. It's us against Ruth and Johnny Sebastian!"

"I don't have any dueling pistols, or swords, and Johnny is a lot bigger than I am," I objected.

"But you're smarter," Midge said. "Remember last summer when we had sort of a war with the Apples? We won against odds. Sending their cat Siegfried up in a balloon was a stroke of genius."

"That was pure accident."

"Well, think of another accident like that!"

I hate to let Midge down and of course there isn't much doubt that I'm smarter than Johnny Sebastian, or Ruth for that matter. But you can't have a flash of genius on order.

After dinner this evening, Uncle Al asked me how business was going and I told him about what had happened.

"You can run into some pretty unethical competition when you get into the business world. It appears to me that you should have got Mrs. Osborn to commit herself when you were first talking to her. That is the first rule of

61

salesmanship—get the customer's signature on the dotted line."

"I don't think she would have signed anything."

"I was just speaking figuratively. Of course you might complain to the F.T.C."

"What's that?" I asked.

"The Federal Trade Commission," Uncle Al said. "I believe it investigates unfair business practices, and if it doesn't there ought to be some government bureau that would look into your complaint. There's a commission or bureau that will poke into everything else."

Uncle Al is a wonderful uncle, but he has a peculiar sense of humor and lots of times he talks in riddles. I wasn't quite sure if he was serious or not.

"Midge thinks we should plan a counterattack," I said. "Make some sort of an accident happen."

"You don't have to plan an accident," Uncle Al said. "Something will happen naturally with you around. Grover's Corner has been quiet for an abnormally long time."

That's another odd thing about Uncle Al. He claims that strange things happen when I'm around. He says the same thing was true of my mother when she was a girl, and that it took Grover's Corner twenty years to recover from her. I asked my mother about it one time and she said Uncle Al has always had odd ideas.

Last year he told me that when mother was a girl she was given a little printing set, so she decided to publish a newspaper. No one in Grover's Corner was interested or took her seriously. She was so angry that she made a tree fall on her guinea-pig pen and released hundreds of guinea pigs, which descended on the houses of Grover's Corner like a plague. Everytime anyone turned around, they almost stepped on, or ran over, a guinea pig. Uncle Al said she was a modern version of the Pied Piper of Hamelin only she did it in reverse—when she played her pipe guinea pigs came from all over to pester everyone in Grover's Corner. I asked Mom about it when I got home and she said Uncle Al told me a very distorted story. A tree branch fell during a windstorm and wrecked her guinea-pig house. There were only twenty-two guinea pigs altogether, and she caught all but three in a few days. As for attracting more guinea pigs, she doesn't even play a musical instrument. Uncle Al can come up with some fantastic stories.

Monday evening, July 19th

This has been a long, hard day but an interesting one. Things are looking up for our baby-sitting business. I'm glad that I didn't plan any accidents as Midge suggested. Uncle Al was right. Just let things take their natural course and they will usually work out.

I was out in the vegetable garden doing some weeding about eleven this morning, when a dilapidated old pickup truck full of wood stopped and an elderly man got out.

"Want to earn a couple of dollars?" he asked.

"Sure! How?"

He jerked his thumb at the load of wood. "I've got to unload that and stack it in a lady's cellar. My legs aren't as young as they used to be. It's just up the road a piece. I'll drop you off on the way back."

"All right. Just let me tell my Aunt Mabel where I'm going."

64

I couldn't find her so I left a note on the kitchen table. I climbed in the cab beside him and we chugged off down the road. I wasn't too happy when he turned into the Osborns'. I was even less happy when we got to the end of the driveway and I saw the Sebastians. Both of them were in the back yard. Ruth seemed to be lecturing the little Osborn girl in a very annoyed manner. Johnny had on swimming trunks and was walking by the edge of the pool with a hose in his hand. He seemed to be washing down the walk around the edge of the pool. There was a long-handled scrub brush lying on the cement. The sides of most pools get dirty at the waterline, and I guess Mrs. Osborn had hired Johnny to clean hers.

Mr. Craig, the man who was delivering the firewood, backed the truck up near a cellar window and we both got out. The cellar window was already open and the hose that Johnny Sebastian was using ran through it. Mr. Craig propped it all the way open with a stick. He squatted down and pointed at a side wall.

"She wants it stacked against that wall. I'll take it off the truck and put it here on the window sill. You go inside and handle that part of the job."

"Too bad that I'm busy at the pool," Johnny said, walking over. "I'd help you otherwise. Looks like a real hot job you got."

I didn't say anything because I couldn't think of a good snappy remark, and also because Johnny is a lot bigger than I am. I went downstairs and began stacking wood. The hose stretched across the basement to a faucet above two laundry tubs. It was about six inches off the floor and I had to step over it every time I carried an armful of wood from the window to the wall.

"Hey, Johnny," I called. "Can I disconnect this hose? It's in the way."

"That's tough," Johnny replied. "I still have some washing down to do."

I pulled on the hose very slowly and managed to get a little slack so that at least it was on the floor. Stacking wood was hot work even though the cellar was cooler than it was outside. Mr. Craig looked about seventy, but he hadn't slowed down much. He pulled the wood off the truck faster than I could carry it away. I tried to keep up, and the harder I worked, the more annoyed I got. If these two Sebastians hadn't been such sneaks, I would have been outside washing down around the pool and falling in every few minutes.

We had been working about twenty minutes when Mr. Wildblood appeared. Mr. Wildblood is a plumber who has fixed things at Uncle Al's. He doesn't look a bit the way you think he would with a name like that. In fact, I think he must be part basset hound. He has big, sad eyes with bags under them, and jowls that hang way down below his jawbone. He usually needs a shave, but Uncle Al says he is the best plumber in the state.

66

" 'Lo, Henry," he said. "Been discovering any oil lately?"

"No," I said, grinning. He was referring to last summer when Midge and I drilled into an old buried oil tank and thought we had discovered oil.

"He says the sump pump won't work," Mr. Wildblood said, grumbling mostly to himself. "Got to be fixed right away. If this summer is like the others have been the last few years, there won't be enough rain to dampen the grass, let alone flood the cellar."

He fussed with the pump for ten or fifteen minutes and finally gave up in disgust. "Guess it would be simpler and quicker to take it back to the shop," he said, and began to disconnect it.

He had the pump removed and was packing up his tools when Johnny Sebastian came over to the window.

"Hey down there, will you turn off the water?" he called.

"My name is not 'Hey down there,'" Mr. Wildblood growled. "And why do you have the hose connected down here in the first place? There's a faucet coming through the foundation around to your left."

"It hasn't any handle on it," Johnny said.

"Guess I better bring a new handle when I bring the pump back," Mr. Wildblood said. "Now just how do you suppose anyone is careless enough to lose a handle off a faucet? That takes some doing."

Mr. Wildblood walked over to the faucet and turned it off. Then he looked at me. I was still stepping over the hose each time with the wood.

"Guess I might as well disconnect it so he can get it out of your way," he said.

He took off the hose. Water began to run out of the end of it so he tossed it over into the pit where the sump pump had been.

"Hey up there!" he called. "Give the hose a minute or two to drain and then coil it up and put it away wherever it belongs."

Johnny Sebastian didn't answer, so Mr. Wildblood called up through the window, "Do you hear me, young fellow?"

"I hear you," Johnny said.

"Don't forget it," Mr. Wildblood said. "Henry's about finished with the wood. When you get the hose out of the way, close that window. Mrs. Osborn won't thank anybody for a basement full of flies."

He picked up his toolbox with one hand and the pump with the other and started toward the stairs.

I finished with the last few sticks of wood and swept up the floor. As I put away the broom I noticed that the sump was half full of water. It was a good-size hole and I stood there looking at it for a minute trying to figure it out. When I went upstairs Johnny was sitting on the side of the pool dangling his feet in the water.

68

"Don't forget what Mr. Wildblood said about putting that hose away and closing the window," I said.

"Mr. Wildblood can go jump in the pool," Johnny said. "I was hired by Mrs. Osborn."

I figured I had done my duty, so I climbed in the truck beside Mr. Craig and we drove off.

"You're a good steady worker," Mr. Craig said, as he let me off at Uncle Al's. "If I get any more orders I'll give you a call."

I thanked him for the two dollars and went inside to take a shower.

I was glad to earn the money, but unloading that wood had proved to me what Uncle Al and Aunt Mabel had said about baby-sitting was true. Baby-sitting has a lot of advantages over other occupations.

After dinner Uncle Al and Aunt Mabel decided to go to the early movie in Princeton and they took Midge and me along. It was almost ten o'clock by the time we started home. On the way we passed the Osborns'. There was water all over the road in front of their house.

"Now what do you suppose all that water is doing out here?" Uncle Al asked. "Pipe burst or something?"

"Maybe Johnny Sebastian contaminated the pool and they're emptying it," Midge suggested.

When we got home we found Mr. Wildblood's truck sitting in the drive.

"Hello, Herb. What are you doing out this time of night

with your truck? I hope my old furnace hasn't blown up."

"Nope. Your neighbor Osborn up the road has about blown up though. The fire department just finished pumping his cellar."

"So that is what all that water was on the road," Uncle Al said. "How could his cellar be full of water, as dry as it is?"

" 'Tain't easy," Mr. Wildblood agreed. "Takes a bit of do-ing."

"Water pipe burst?" Uncle Al asked.

"Nothing that simple," Mr. Wildblood said. "What a mess that basement was. You know that wood you stacked down in the basement today, Henry?"

I nodded.

"Well, it was floating all over the basement. Practically a log jam down there."

"Didn't he have a sump pump?" Uncle Al asked.

"He had one but it wasn't working," Mr. Wildblood replied. "I took it back to the shop to repair it. That puts me in a bit of a spot. Henry, there was a boy in the back yard washing down around the pool."

"Johnny Sebastian."

"I knew it was Johnny something. Now I want you to tell me exactly what happened as I was leaving. What I said and what I did."

"Johnny yelled down to you to turn off the water. You did, and disconnected the hose and called up to him to coil it up and put it away. He didn't answer. You called to him again, and this time he said he'd heard you. You told him to close the window so flies wouldn't get into the basement."

"That checks with what I remember," Mr. Wildblood said. "What did I do with the hose when I disconnected it?"

"Dropped it down into the hole where the pump had been," I said.

"Did that boy Johnny Sebastian coil up the hose?"

"He hadn't when I left," I said. I began to grin.

"What are you grinning about?" Mr. Wildblood asked. "You know what happened, don't you?"

Mr. Wildblood and I both began to laugh. "Craziest

thing I ever heard of," Mr. Wildblood said. "How come that kid didn't notice after an hour or two? The water level in that pool had to be going down. Wonder he didn't dive in and break his skull."

"Maybe he did notice and couldn't figure it out," I said.

"He didn't look like the brightest kid in the world," Mr. Wildblood agreed. "And it must have been sort of mystifying." He began to laugh again, this time so hard that he had to stop and wipe his eyes.

"Look, if one of you two geniuses would tell the rest of us what happened, we could all laugh," Uncle Al said.

"You tell them, Henry," Mr. Wildblood said.

"Johnny didn't turn off the nozzle at his end of the hose and I guess he must have dropped it into the pool. The floor of the basement is a lot lower than the water in the pool, and since the hose was full of water, it started siphoning the water from the pool into the basement."

"You've studied your physics," Mr. Wildblood said. "You hit it right on the head."

"Superb! Absolutely superb!" Midge said. "Do you mean that goofy Johnny Sebastian emptied the pool into the basement?"

"Well, I'd call it an accident," Mr. Wildblood said. "Only if he'd put away the hose as he was told, or even if he'd been half awake, it wouldn't have happened."

"Was there much damage?" Uncle Al asked.

"Mainly just a mess. The cellar will be damp for a while

and the oil burner's motor was under water. I've got it in back here and I'll dry it out and make any necessary repairs free of charge, since I feel partly responsible."

"Don't see why you should."

"The Osborns deserve just what they got," Midge said. "Hiring that cheap competition to do their baby-sitting."

"I think maybe they've learned their lesson," Mr. Wildblood said. "Mrs. Osborn asked me to have Henry call her about tomorrow."

"I better go do that," I said.

Midge followed me into the house while Aunt Mabel and Uncle Al stayed outside talking to Mr. Wildblood.

"That was a positive stroke of genius, Henry," Midge said as I looked up the Osborn number.

"I didn't touch a thing, I swear," I said.

"Brilliant planning," Midge said. "There's only one thing you could have done better. You should have arranged it so the pool would empty into the Sebastians' basement."

There's not much use arguing with Midge when she gets an idea. I called the Osborns' number and got Mrs. Osborn. She explained that Ruth Sebastian would be unable to baby-sit any more and she would appreciate it very much if the firm of Reed and Glass could take over the contract. I said I'd be there shortly before ten the next morning.

Midge said she'd take the afternoon shift and went

74

home very happy because we'd come out ahead of Ruth and Johnny Sebastian.

I was on my way upstairs when Uncle Al came in.

"I'm glad to see events have borne out my predictions," he said. "Just let things take their course and something's bound to happen. It reminds me of the time when your mother was a tiny girl and she was hoping and praying that it would snow so there would be no school the next day. There was something very important she would miss if she had to go to school. As it turned out it didn't snow, but there was an accident and no school."

"What happened?"

"It was her turn to bring something in for what they called 'Show and Tell.' She took a pet skunk."

Tuesday evening, July 20th

I have just finished my first day of baby-sitting at the Osborns'. I've never been so tired in my life. I don't know whether we won a victory over the Sebastians or not.

The little Osborn girl's name is Belinda. I looked it up in the dictionary a few minutes ago and it comes from an old Italian word meaning a serpent. I suppose it was the most accurate name they could find, but it doesn't half do that little monster justice. . . . She's a fiend!

Belinda isn't mischievous like Danny Wittenberg. I can stand that. Belinda likes to torture baby-sitters. She has only one trick, but that's all she needs to make life miserable.

I arrived at the Osborns' shortly before ten, as I had promised. Mrs. Osborn showed me around the house, told me about lunch, kissed Belinda good-by, and hurried off to the peace of the gift shop.

"Well, what would you like to do, Belinda?" I asked, trying to sound very friendly.

It wasn't easy to sound cheery and friendly because she had been staring at me through those thick-lensed glasses from the minute I arrived. She didn't say anything, and there was no expression on her face. I had begun to think she was retarded and couldn't talk, but Mrs. Osborn hadn't mentioned anything like that. Finally, after asking the same question three times, I got an answer.

"I want a drink of water," she said.

"Okay," I said. "You know where the glasses are and where the water spigot is. Help yourself."

I didn't mind getting her a drink of water, but my theory is that you shouldn't pamper little kids.

I should have followed her into the kitchen, but naturally I didn't realize what was going on in her scheming little mind. I was looking through a magazine so I continued to look at it for a minute or two longer. Then I walked back to the kitchen. She was gone.

"Belinda!" I said. "Where are you?"

There was no answer but I didn't think much about it. I went to the back door and looked in the back yard. She was no place to be seen.

"Belinda!" I called. "Answer me!"

There was a dead silence. I went back inside and carefully went from room to room with no success. I began to get worried. I went outside and walked completely

around the house. Then I looked in the garage and in the little house over the filter system at the pool. The garden-house door was latched from the outside, so I skipped that. The Osborns have a big yard with lots of shrubs and evergreens. I looked around most of these before I went inside. Belinda had simply vanished. I decided to go through the house again. This time I looked in every closet. I don't like looking in people's closets because I don't think it's polite, but this was an emergency. I opened every door in that entire house and there was no Belinda. Finally I looked down in the cellar. The cellar was certainly a mess with pools of water all over and wood scattered everywhere. I waded over and looked in the furnace room but there was no one.

By this time I was really worried. I began to think of kidnapers. She might have walked out to the road and have been picked up by someone. Of course I didn't really know Belinda yet or I would have realized how silly that thought was. No one in his right mind would want to have her.

There was the possibility that she might have gone outside and set off through the woods. The Osborns' house, like all the others along that road, backed up on farm and woodland. I decided the only thing to do was to call Mrs. Osborn and explain that inside of ten minutes I had managed to lose her only child. Of course, if I were her I'd be relieved at news like that, but mothers are peculiar.

I had dialed two of the numbers when I heard the water running. I put down the telephone and rushed to the kitchen. There was Belinda, getting a drink of water.

"Where have you been?" I demanded.

"Getting a drink of water," she said. "Where have you been?"

I felt like taking her glass of water and pouring it over her head, but I kept control of myself and acted like a gentleman.

"Where were you when I was looking all over for you?"

"I've been right here," she said, without changing her expression.

"You weren't any such thing," I said sternly. I can look very stern when I try.

"I was so!"

Nothing would shake her from her story. I tried being

jolly and pretending that I thought it had all been fun, but it didn't budge her a bit.

"You win," I said. "It was very smart. Tell me how you did it."

"I was right here," she said, staring at me with those black eyes of hers. With her long stringy black hair she began to look more and more like a witch. I haven't seen many witches with big thick spectacles, but I can tell you it doesn't improve their looks a bit.

I still don't know what happened. There are front and back stairs to the house, and possibly she could have followed me up and down and around, keeping out of sight. That would have been difficult though, because there is a door to the back stairs and it squeaked when it opened. Then I thought of the doors under the sink. I didn't let on to her and I didn't open them at the time. Later in the day I opened them and looked. There were several buckets, some boxes of soap powder, some sponges, and odds and ends. There might have been room for a little girl to squeeze in, but it would have been a tight squeeze. Midge believes in the witch theory. She claims that Belinda changed herself into a mop and stood in the corner. She does look a little bit like a mop but there has to be some more logical explanation.

"We'll go outside," I said. This time I didn't ask, I told her.

It was a beautiful sunny day. I spotted a croquet set and asked Belinda if she wanted to play a game. She didn't answer, but nodded her head. One wicket was missing but I found it and we began to play.

For a five-year-old she wasn't too bad a player. I won one game and let her win one. Then about halfway through the third game, I knocked her ball out of bounds. It went over behind a spreading yew. Just as she went after it a car came roaring down the highway, sounding like an airplane. I turned to see what it was, and when I turned back Belinda was gone. I strolled casually over to the yew and then suddenly dashed around it. She wasn't there. There were a number of shrubs and bushes and she could have been behind any one of them. I began looking, walking very quietly, pausing every few steps to listen. That infuriating kid had vanished again.

I wasn't worried this time. I didn't think about kidnapers, and I figured that sooner or later she'd come back —but I was annoyed. I couldn't let the little black-haired fiend think she was smarter than I was. A baby-sitter has to maintain respect, and he can't do that if the baby thinks he or she is smarter than the sitter.

I tried flopping on the ground and looking under the bushes, but that didn't do any good. Then I went in the house to get a drink of water and peeked out from behind the curtain. Nothing moved in the back yard except a robin and a sparrow. Finally I went back and started to finish the game by myself. I had made about three shots when I heard her behind me.

"It isn't your turn," she said.

"Anyone who isn't ready to play after a lapse of thirty seconds loses his turn," I said. "Rule forty-six, page 19."

That sounded very official and she didn't question it. She stayed around to play the rest of the game and I felt I'd won at least one little skirmish of the war.

I had no more trouble until lunch time. I asked her what she wanted and she said "Peanut butter and jelly sandwich" just as I might have expected. I made it and cut it into two pieces.

"That's not the way Mommy makes it," she said, staring at me. "I won't eat it."

"What's wrong with it?"

"She cuts it another way. It's prettier and it fits my mouth better."

I finally figured out that she wanted the sandwich cut into two rectangles. If I hadn't hated peanut butter and jelly sandwiches so, I might have eaten it and made her another one.

"It's in little pieces by the time it reaches your stomach," I told her. "And no matter how I slice it, it's still peanut butter and jelly. Eat it and quit complaining."

She stared at me so hard that I figured she was trying to cast a voodoo spell and turn me into a zombie, but I pre-

84

tended not to notice and made myself two decent sandwiches with meat in them.

"What would you like to drink?" I asked.

"Coca-Cola," she said. "Let's eat outside. I'll take the sandwiches."

I should have suspected that she wasn't being co-operative without a sneaky reason. I got two bottles of Coke and went out to the patio. She was nowhere in sight. This time I didn't bother looking for her. I sat down on one of the chairs and tried to figure out where she had gone. Meanwhile I drank my Coke. I was hungry and I wanted her to come back with the sandwiches, but I didn't move at all. I finished my Coke and started on hers. I thought that might bring her, but it didn't. Finally I got so hungry I couldn't stand it any longer. I went inside and made myself another sandwich.

When I got outside, there she was with the plate of sandwiches sitting on the table. She was eating hers and my two were still on the plate.

"Are you going to eat three sandwiches?" she asked.

I did my best not to choke and said, "Yes, I'm going to eat three. You were so long getting here that I got even hungrier. I also drank your Coke. What did you do? Lose your way?"

"I've been here all the time waiting for you," she said.

About one o'clock Midge appeared, to take over for the afternoon. I got her off to one side and warned her about

Belinda. I would have liked to have had a swim, but the pool wasn't full yet. Instead, I went down in the basement and restacked the wood. When I finished I went up to the back yard and there was Belinda sitting like a little angel a few feet from Midge. Midge was reading a book.

"I think you exaggerated," Midge said. "Or else you just don't inspire confidence."

"Wait," I warned. About the only thing I wanted to inspire in Belinda, after the morning I had put in, was terror.

I got on my bike and started home. The fire department had pumped the cellar out onto the driveway and it had run down onto the road. The asphalt made a dip right in front of the Osborns' house and there was still a big puddle of water from the night before. I had just turned onto the main road when a car came tearing along. I got over on the shoulder, but the car swooped toward me and went through the edge of the puddle. Water splashed all over me.

Of course it was the red MG, with Ruth Sebastian driving. This was the second time exactly the same thing had happened. The first time had been after a rain and there were puddles all up and down the road. But this puddle in front of the Osborns' was probably the only one within five miles. There was something strange about her being in the right place at the right time in that little red car.

I had been home an hour or so when Midge called to

say that Belinda had vanished. "I'm getting worried, she's been gone so long."

"She'll come back," I said. "And when she does, she'll make you so mad that you'll wish she hadn't."

Midge stopped by on her way home at six. She looked tired and disgusted.

"We've got to think of something to outwit that child!" Midge said. "It's humiliating, that's what it is. I was reading her a story and in the middle of it she was gone. I looked for forty-five minutes. Then suddenly she was back in her chair and complaining because I had taken so long. She actually insisted that I had gone to get a drink of water and she was anxious to finish the story. Henry, you've got to think of something!"

"Like what?"

"If I knew what, I'd think of it myself," Midge said. "But if we don't do something I go on strike."

Friday, July 23rd

The time has gone by fast since Tuesday. I've been busy. Our baby-sitting service is becoming very well known and we have a number of jobs scheduled for the next several weeks. The Henry Reed Baby-Sitting Service is probably the best-known organization of its kind in New Jersey and maybe even in the east. I'll bet it's the only one that advertises on the radio.

I had a call Wednesday morning from a Mrs. Adams who lives up the road, a short distance this side of the Osborns. She wanted to know if I could come take care of her boy Craig for several hours, starting about ten o'clock, while she went shopping in Trenton. Her husband, she explained, was still in bed and I was to keep Craig quiet if such a thing was possible. Craig is a little tow-headed bundle of energy about five years old. I took one look at him and decided that keeping him quiet for any length of time wasn't going to be easy.

"It's a nice day," I suggested. "We might take a hike across the fields to the woods over by the creek."

"Marvelous idea," Mrs. Adams agreed. "I'll make you some sandwiches."

In less than ten minutes we were hiking across the fields and she was on her way to Trenton. I was sorry that I hadn't brought Agony, but it was just as well. Agony scares away most of the animals and birds and you don't get a chance to look at them closely. We had a great time looking at crayfish, frogs, birds, and animals. My Uncle Al says my mother should have been a naturalist and that she has always preferred bugs to people. That's not really true, but she does like all sorts of wild life, and so do I. Craig is a very intelligent boy and was interested in what I told him about the things we saw.

When we got back to the house we found Mr. Adams in the kitchen cooking bacon and eggs for himself. We'd had our lunch, but we sat down and had some orange juice, and toast and jelly.

"We saw a bug that walks on water, two frogs, a rabbit, a squirrel, and a woodcock," Craig said. "Betcha you never saw a woodcock."

"Can't say I have," Mr. Adams admitted.

"Hank told me all about everything we saw," Craig said. "He's smart and knows all about animals and birds."

"You seem to have made quite a hit, Hank," Mr. Adams said. "I don't know how much you know about animals, but you're pretty smart when it comes to small boys. A ten mile hike is just what this chap needs to keep him from wrecking the place. No other baby-sitter ever thought of it though."

"Woodcocks have long bills," Craig said. "And long legs. Hank says they're good eating. Want to go see one?"

"Can't. The station just called and I have to run over there for a couple of hours," Mr. Adams said. "Could you stay until about three-thirty, Hank?"

"Sure," I agreed.

"My daddy runs the new radio station," Craig announced.

"I don't run it, but I am part of the staff," Mr. Adams said. "That's why I slept so late this morning."

"Are you an announcer?" I asked.

"I'm the advertising manager," Mr. Adams said. "But last night I was filling in as announcer. Getting a new station under way is an interesting experience, but a lot of work. Don't want to advertise your baby-sitting service on the air, do you?"

The idea sounded interesting. "I might," I said. "How much would it cost?"

Mr. Adams took a sip of his coffee and looked out the window. For a minute I thought he hadn't heard me. Then he got a funny look on his face.

90

"That's not a bad idea," he said. "We've got lots of unfilled advertising time, being such a new station. Advertising a baby-sitting service is right in line with our policy of service to our listening public. And we would be the first station to carry the advertising of a baby-sitting enterprise —Henry, I'll make you a deal. Baby-sit the next three hours for free and I'll give you several spot announcements over our station."

I didn't see how I could lose, so I agreed. Mr. Adams took down a few facts such as my name and Midge's, where we both lived, our telephone numbers, and what our rates were.

"Got any special qualifications?" he asked.

"Well, I passed the lifesaving course in Naples," I said.

"Naples? What were you doing in Naples?"

"My father works for the government—diplomatic service. I've lived most of my life in Europe. I'd rather live in Grover's Corner."

"I suppose you would," Mr. Adams said. "Speak Italian?"

"Pretty well. I speak French better though."

"Excellent. Any other special qualifications?"

"My partner Midge, I mean Margaret, has had experience in ballet," I said.

"Good qualification," Mr. Adams said, glancing at his watch. "Look, I've got to run. I'll turn on the radio for you and get my station. Listen to some of the spot announcements and maybe you'll get an idea of something special you want to say. If you do, give me a call."

He hurried out to his car and drove off. Craig was tired after all our walking and he went off to take a nap. I had very little to do but listen to the radio. I don't want to criticize Mr. Adams, and he probably didn't write most of them, but the advertisements didn't seem to have much punch. There was one singing commercial that was catchy. It advertised a reducing machine sold by a man named Duffy and went, "If you feel fat and puffy, the man to see is Duffy." I decided I could think of something as good as anything I'd heard. However, when I tried I found it wasn't as easy as I'd expected. I didn't have what I'd call a flash of genius, but I had one idea just before Craig woke from his nap. I called Mr. Adams at his station.

"Not bad at all, Hank," he said. "In fact I think that can be worked into quite a flashy piece of copy. We happen to have a girl here this afternoon who can play the piano and sing. We'll get her to tape it. You listen at eight in the morning."

Mrs. Adams came home about three-thirty. I charged her only from ten to twelve-thirty and explained that I had made an arrangement with her husband for the other three hours.

Midge wasn't back from her ballet lesson when I got home. Aunt Mabel, Uncle Al, and I went out to dinner so

92

I forgot all about telling Midge about our advertisement until the next morning. I called her just in time. The Glasses eat breakfast about the same time we do, so I guess all of us were having our second slice of toast.

I had told Aunt Mabel and Uncle Al that I wanted to hear a special commercial about eight, but I didn't tell them whose. For several minutes I thought Mr. Adams had forgotten me because the ad didn't come on at eight but at five minutes after eight, right after the news. It started with a girl playing the piano and singing:

"Mary had a little lamb,
Little lamb, little lamb.
Mary had a little lamb,
It's fleece was white as snow.

Everywhere that Mary went,
Mary went, Mary went,
Everywhere that Mary went
The lamb was sure to go.

It followed her to school one day,
School one day, school one day.
It followed her to school one day,
Which was against the rule."

Then the music stopped and a man spoke. It sounded like Mr. Adams.

"Folks, Mary wouldn't have much trouble today. Her education wouldn't be interrupted by her little lamb's following her to school. Because she would simply telephone the Henry Reed Baby-Sitting Service, and in the twitch of a lamb's tail, a competent baby-sitter would be there. Henry Reed and his partner Miss Margaret Glass offer reliable, efficient baby-sitting at prices you can afford. Call Henry at HA 9-1234 or Margaret at HA 9-1763. If your little lamb wants to learn to dance, Margaret can teach him ballet. If you want your child to be able to communicate with your French poodle—or possibly call General de Gaulle—Henry can coach him in French. If you live in the Grover's Corner area and you need a baby-sitter for a lion or a lamb call Henry Reed's Baby-Sitting Service!"

"That ought to bring some results," Uncle Al said, scratching his ear. "I'm not sure what kind of results, but I predict something will happen."

Nothing much happened except that the telephone rang most of the morning. Advertising certainly pays, but I should have had a bigger organization. I needed a staff all over New Jersey, eastern Pennsylvania, and southern New York. A lot of people didn't pay any attention to the "Grover's Corner area." I had three calls from Trenton, one from New Brunswick, and one from a woman in Altoona, Pennsylvania, who got mad at me when I explained that Grover's Corner was in New Jersey and not just outside Altoona. She wanted me to pay for her call. Then some man called from Asbury Park and wanted to know if I was the Henry Reed who mended Oriental rugs.

Midge came over about noon and we compared notes. Fourteen people had called, including two who had asked for her, said "Baa! Baa! Baa!" and then hung up. She thinks a boy she knows in school was responsible.

We did get four jobs from the announcement though. One on Thursday morning, one on Thursday afternoon, one today, and one for next week.

Saturday, July 24th

They had our advertisement on the radio again yesterday afternoon, last night, and this morning. Midge and I have lots of work lined up. Everybody has heard about us. Midge said two people stopped her on the street in Princeton today and asked her if she was the Margaret Glass they had heard about on the radio.

"You're famous," Uncle Al said at breakfast when he heard the advertisement again. "And that's not easy in Princeton. We've got geniuses of all sizes and shapes and descriptions—atomic scientists, famous literary figures, well-known economists, writers, historians, musicians, not to mention the governor of New Jersey. I think you've had more publicity than he has in the last two days."

"I guess I'll have to grow long hair or a beard or something so I'll look like a celebrity," I said.

"No, I've discovered the famous ones look fairly normal," Uncle Al said. "The oddballs are those who hope someone will think they're famous. The smart thing to do when you are well known is to be as inconspicuous as possible."

The mailman came by while we were talking and I went out for the mail. I glanced at it and saw that there was no letter from my mother, and gave it to Uncle Al. He was at the breakfast table having his second or third cup of coffee.

"This illustrates what I mean," he said, handing me a folder, or sort of booklet. "You're now so famous that the Internal Revenue Service has heard of you."

The booklet looked very official. The title of it was "Federal Employment Tax Forms." Beneath the title it said, "This package contains Form 7018, Form w-2, Form w-4, Form 941A, and Publication No. 213." It certainly looked complicated. I read one paragraph which said, "This package has been designed to give you supplies of several forms you need to comply with the laws relating to income tax withholding and social security (F.I.C.A.) taxes."

"What's this all about?" I asked.

"Well, it means your troubles are starting," Uncle Al said, glancing at the booklet. "You're the head of a business enterprise and you've got to worry about these things. Pretty soon you'll need another employee just to fill out

97

forms. Let's see now, income tax witholding, social security, unemployment compensation, disability insurance, hospitalization—by the time you get all these deducted from your pay, you'll be lucky if you have money to keep your bicycle in repair."

"Be serious, Al," Aunt Mabel said. "Henry won't owe any taxes unless he earns a lot more than I think he will. I don't understand why the form was sent to him in the first place. Where did they get his name? And what should he do with that?"

"Ignore it," Uncle Al said. "You aren't running the sort of business that has to make out those returns. And unless you make more than six hundred dollars a year you don't have to make out an income tax return."

"If I made six hundred dollars I'd ride around in a Rolls-Royce, not on a bicycle," I said.

"Well, I doubt that," Uncle Al said. "Even without taxes it wouldn't be much more than a beat-up Volkswagen for six hundred dollars. Anyhow, just pretend you don't exist as far as the Internal Revenue Service is concerned. Once they have your name in their files it takes years to convince them that you don't owe them money. If you start writing to them you'll spend a fortune in postage. Before you get things straightened out, you'll be a taxpayer."

He tossed the booklet in the wastepaper basket, which seemed like a waste of government money for paper and printing. I got it out and wrote "return to sender" on it the way they do when mail is sent to the wrong address. I dropped it in the mailbox on my way to a baby-sitting job.

Tuesday night, July 27th

I didn't do any baby-sitting Sunday. The Glasses were invited to the beach for the day by some friends who have a cottage near Beach Haven. They took me along. It was a beautiful day and the water was just right. Midge and I swam and loafed in the sun all day.

It was a good thing I got rested on Sunday because I certainly needed all the energy I could find Monday morning. I've heard about Blue Monday, but no one really knows what a blue Monday is until he's had a job baby-sitting with a fiend like Belinda Osborn.

I had a brilliant idea and took Agony with me. That wasn't easy because Agony, being a beagle, isn't the fastest runner in the world. He's built fairly close to the ground and also he's fat. Aunt Mabel feeds him so much that he looks like a sausage. About a third of the way to the Osborns he began to fall behind and puff like a steamboat. I stopped and put him in the basket on my bicycle. That was fine for a short distance, and then he saw a rabbit or something that made him jump up and whirl about. I went in the ditch and both of us were dumped. I had two other close calls but finally I got there.

Agony loves to chase a ball. If you will throw it for him, he'll go fetch all day long. Once you start he'll pester you for an hour. My scheme worked perfectly—for a while. I got Belinda to throw the ball for Agony a few times. She enjoyed it for a while. When she got a little tired of the game, I managed to stick the ball in my pocket without either her or Agony seeing me. Just as I expected, Agony kept tagging her around, waiting for her to produce the ball and throw it. Every few minutes he would bark to tell her he was still waiting. I sat down and relaxed; I got out a paperback, *The Time Machine* by H. G. Wells, and began reading. I felt a lot better. At least I wasn't being outsmarted by a little first grader.

Belinda was mad as a hornet. Several times she started to slip away and Agony tagged after her, barking happily. Finally she came over and stood in front of me solemnly and without blinking for at least a minute.

"What kind of a dog is he?" she asked.

"A beagle. They're wonderful rabbit dogs."

"Do you mean they hunt rabbits?"

"That's right."

"Can we go rabbit-hunting, Agony and me?"

"If you stay right on your property."

"Come on, Agony, let's go hunting," she shouted.

Together they disappeared around the corner of the garage. Several minutes went by and I began to feel uneasy. Then I heard Agony bark and went back to my book. The trouble was, he kept on barking. Finally his bark became a yip and I knew something was wrong. I stuck my book in my pocket and hurried around the garage. There was Agony locked up tight. She'd taken him rabbit-hunting all right and had locked him in a rabbit pen. There wasn't much chance of his catching a rabbit though, because the pen hadn't been used for at least a year.

She was gone almost an hour. Even though I'd been through the game before, I couldn't help worrying. Baby-sitting is certainly a responsibility. There're so many things that can happen to a five- or six-year-old, especially one like Belinda. They've suffocated in cleaning bags, locked themselves in old refrigerators, and fallen off roofs. I spent half my time worrying that something terrible had happened to her and the other half thinking nothing was too terrible to serve her right.

I looked everywhere, checking the pool every five minutes to make certain that she hadn't fallen in. Agony was no help at all. I kept saying, "Let's find Belinda, Agony," but he gave a disgusted sniff and wandered off toward the back of the yard, looking for a rabbit.

She finally came back on her own just as she had done before. As usual she pretended she hadn't been gone at all, which made it twice as annoying.

"We didn't catch any rabbits," she said.

"So I notice. Look, if you don't stop this disappearing act, I'm going to lock you in that pen the way you did Agony."

I don't know whether she believed me or not, but I don't think I scared her very much.

Belinda did have one nice trait. She took long naps. Right after lunch she decided to go to sleep in the hammock in the back yard. She was sleeping soundly when Midge came at one to take the afternoon shift. It seemed safe to leave her, so Midge walked to the road with me while I explained that Agony hadn't worked too well. We were trying to think of something to try next when Ruth Sebastian drove by in her little red car. When she saw us, she came to a stop and backed up.

"What's the matter? Has little Belinda disappeared and the famous Henry Reed Baby-Sitting Service can't find her?"

"I don't know what you mean," Midge said. "Belinda is in the back yard."

"I'll bet," Ruth said. "I couldn't stand that child, which

is why I quit and recommended you two. I hope you don't mind. Well, happy hunting!"

She drove off before Midge could answer, which is just as well. When Midge finally got through sputtering she said, "This is the end, absolutely the living end. So Ruth Sebastian is going around saying she quit and stuck us with a fiend we can't keep track of! Henry, this is a crisis, a real honest-to-goodness crisis! We've got to do something or the reputation of the Henry Reed Baby-Sitting Service will be ruined!"

I didn't like the situation any better than Midge did, but I couldn't think of anything except possibly to put Belinda in chains. I called to Agony and went pedaling down the road. This time I went very slowly so he could keep up with me. He was panting like a steam engine by the time I reached the Adams house, so I stopped to let him rest. Craig saw me and came out.

"Tell your father the advertisments were wonderful," I said.

"He's down in his workshop if you want to tell him," Craig said.

That seemed a good idea so I followed Craig to the basement. Mr. Adams was puttering around with a lot of electronic equipment that looked very interesting, so I stayed quite a while. As I was leaving he showed me a little walkie-talkie set that was no bigger than two little battery radios.

"They're good for about a quarter of a mile," Mr. Adams said. "More a toy than anything, although Craig and I have found them useful when we've gone fishing together. You know, when we're fishing a small stream where there's no danger from deep water, I can let him be off by himself and still keep in touch."

"Would you rent those to me for a few hours?" I asked Mr. Adams. "They might be the solution to a tough baby-sitting problem."

"You're welcome to use them at no cost. Just bring them back in good shape."

I hurried on home with Agony yelping dismally as he lost ground. I telephoned Midge as soon as I got in the house and explained what I had in mind.

"I want to add an extra touch," Midge said. "Go over to our garage and you'll find one of those polished metal balls that people put on pedestals on the lawn. Somebody gave it to Mom one time and she's never used it. Bring it with you. If you get here fast you can get all set while Belinda is still asleep."

I left Agony with Aunt Mabel and went to Midge's for the metal globe. Then I pedaled to the Osborns' as fast as I could. Belinda was still asleep so I made a quick survey of the back yard. A big maple tree seemed the most likely spot. I gave one of the walkie-talkies to Midge and with the other in my pocket I climbed the tree. Midge had to give me a boost to reach the first limb, but after that it was simple. The leaves were so thick that it wasn't easy to find a location where I could see reasonably well in all directions, but finally I found a spot.

"I'm all set," I said into the walkie-talkie. "Testing—one, two, three—can you read me?"

"Loud and clear," Midge said. "Maybe too loud and clear. She might be able to hear you without a receiver."

We did a little experimenting and found that we could talk in scarcely more than a whisper and still hear each other perfectly.

"Why don't you go and make some noise so she'll wake up?" I suggested. "Perching up in this tree is going to be uncomfortable after a while."

"Gladly," Midge said. "I'm looking forward to this." She disappeared and a few minutes later came back with Belinda trailing behind her. Midge had carefully placed the metal globe in the center of the lawn. Belinda spotted it immediately.

"What's that?" she asked.

"My crystal ball," Midge said.

"What's it for?"

"I can look into that and see things. I can tell what's happening in faraway places. I brought it so that I can look in it and tell where you are when you run away and hide."

Belinda didn't say a word. She had her back toward me

but I knew she was staring at Midge with that peculiar stare of hers, plotting something.

"So if you want to do your runaway act, go right ahead," Midge said. "I'm going to sit down in this chair and relax."

She sat down and closed her eyes. Belinda stood watching her for several minutes. Then she marched over and stared at the crystal ball. She must not have seen anything to scare her because she promptly began a slow circle of Midge's chair. When she was directly behind Midge she backed slowly toward the corner of the house. By the time she got to the corner she was out of Midge's sight but I could still see her from my perch in the tree. There was an enormous spreading yew near the drive and she ducked under one of the branches and disappeared into the center of it.

"Midge from sky lookout," I whispered into the walkie-talkie. "Come in, please."

"I'm in," Midge said. "Where is she?"

"Around the corner of the house, hiding in the middle of that big spreading yew by the driveway."

"Good," Midge said. "I'll discombobulate her."

She picked up the big metal ball and began walking around the back yard. She moved over to where she could be seen by Belinda but turned her back toward the yew.

"Crystal ball, tell me where Belinda is hiding!" she said

in a loud voice, holding one hand to her forehead. She didn't look much like a gypsy fortuneteller since she was wearing shorts instead of long flowing robes, but otherwise her act was pretty good.

"I see something. I see something!" she announced. "The picture is becoming clearer. I see a little girl hiding in a yew near the driveway. I also see a bee buzzing over the tree. It is going to sting her if she doesn't quit hiding and get back where she belongs."

The yew began to shake and a minute later Belinda appeared. She looked as though she would like to murder

Midge, but she didn't say a word. Midge put the ball back on the lawn and sat down in her chair again.

"Would you like to play a game or go swimming?" she suggested.

"No!"

"All right," Midge said. "Do anything you like."

Belinda stood looking at the ball for about five minutes. Whatever else Belinda is, she isn't dumb. There was an empty plastic bucket sitting just outside the garden tool house. Belinda marched over, picked it up, and returned to the center of the lawn. She looked at Midge to be certain that she wasn't being watched and then put the bucket upside down over the ball. After hesitating a minute she slowly sidled toward the garage.

"She just put a bucket over your crystal ball," I said.

"The crystal ball will see everything, bucket or no bucket," Midge said softly. "Where's she going?"

"She just disappeared into the garage," I said. "I don't know whether you know it or not, but there's a little loft at the back end of the garage. I can't see it but she may climb up there."

"Okay!" Midge answered. "Madam Glass will now go into one of her famous trances."

"Belinda, it's no use," she called. "If you don't come back immediately I'll have to consult my crystal ball again. And putting that bucket over it doesn't do a thing."

Belinda wasn't convinced. She didn't stir. Midge picked up the ball and walked around the yard with it in her hand. When she got over in front of the garage she said, "I begin to see a picture. It's cloudy, but it's becoming clearer. I can make out a little girl hiding in a garage."

She had been speaking in a deep, sort of ghostly voice. She dropped the ghostly tone and said in a very sharp voice, "Belinda, come right out of the garage immediately before I come in after you." She put some real authority in her voice and sounded just like Mrs. Houghton, our history teacher, does when she is annoyed.

Belinda came out of the garage a minute later, her chin down almost to her chest. She looked unhappy.

"Want to go swimming?" Midge asked.

"No."

"All right, try running away and hiding, if you'd rather," Midge said, flopping in her chair.

Belinda went back to staring at the metal ball. She was thinking hard and she had a real inspiration this time. She picked up the crystal ball and made off with it. I was laughing so hard that for a minute I forgot to watch and almost lost her. Finally, I saw her as she disappeared around the edge of the little garden tool house. A second later I saw the end of a board swing out and drop back again. I didn't actually see Belinda disappear, but I had a good idea of what had happened.

I did an imitation of Dracula and said into my walkie-talkie, "The crystal ball sees everything but who can see the crystal ball?"

"What are you talking about?" Midge asked.

"She hooked your crystal ball and headed for the hills. Now what are you going to do?"

"This requires a little thought," Midge said. "I hope you saw where she went."

"Around the back of the little garden house," I said. "I think we've solved a mystery and found her Number One place. My guess is that there is a loose board on the back. It's nailed at the top. She pulls that out and slips inside. When you see the doors locked you don't think about looking inside. That's where she's probably been several times when I couldn't find her."

"I'm going into my act," Midge said.

"I hope she doesn't keep this up much longer," I said. "I'm beginning to feel pretty cramped up here. I never knew maples had such hard branches."

"Belinda, have you disappeared again?" Midge called out in an annoyed voice. "Come back here!"

Naturally Belinda didn't answer. I could picture her, hunched down in the tool house, clutching that crystal ball.

"And it won't do you a bit of good, taking my crystal ball," Midge said sternly. "It can send messages to me for almost a mile."

In case Belinda was looking through a crack in the tool house, Midge went through the whole act of putting her head in her hands and concentrating.

"I begin to get a message," she said slowly. "It's very distant and dim but I see a little girl running around in back of a garden tool house carrying a crystal ball. I can't quite make out what she's doing now, but it looks like she is pulling at a loose board and slipping inside the house.

That must be it, you're hiding in the garden tool house."

She walked over and opened the door. "Get up off that dirty floor or your clothes will be ruined and your mother will be furious!" Midge said sternly. "And give me back that ball!"

Belinda was beaten. She didn't march out sullenly as she had before, but she walked back very quietly and meekly beside Midge.

"Let's not have any more of this silly hiding," Midge said.

"Can anybody else read your crystal ball?" Belinda asked in a hopeful voice.

"Henry can, and I'm going to advise him to bring it unless you promise me you'll not hide anymore," Midge said. "As a matter of fact, I think I'll send Henry a message through the crystal ball. I'm going to ask him to come nail that board back where it belongs and to take a swim."

For a minute I thought Belinda was going to cry, but she's tough. Midge walked a short distance away from her.

"I'll make some excuse for walking around the house," Midge said into the walkie-talkie. "You get down and appear in a few minutes. We might as well give her the full treatment."

I didn't hear what she told Belinda but a minute later they disappeared around the corner of the house. I got down as fast as I could and went after them. I circled the house behind them until they got back by the pool. Then I strolled in along the drive.

"I got your message," I said. "So I hurried right over."

"You sure did," Midge said. "You must have flown."

"What's this about a board you want nailed?"

"There's a loose board on the garden tool house," Midge said. "Belinda and I think it ought to be nailed down— don't we, Belinda?"

"I guess so," Belinda said, without too much enthusiasm.

I found a hammer and nails in the basement and nailed the board back where it belonged. I'd brought my bathing suit earlier, so I changed and we all went swimming. We had a good time and Belinda behaved herself except once when she thought we weren't looking and kicked the crystal ball into the pool. I doubt if we'll have any more trouble with her. The Henry Reed Baby-Sitting Service is not an outfit to tamper with.

Thursday, July 29th

You meet some interesting people when you're baby-sitting, and now and then you do some interesting things. Last night I went camping and baby-sitting at the same time. It isn't often you can get paid for going camping.

I got a call yesterday morning from Mrs. Adams. She and Mr. Adams had been invited to a big affair in New York which included dinner and a theater party. They didn't expect to get back much before one-thirty A.M. I wasn't crazy about riding home on my bicycle at one-thirty in the morning, but business is business and it was too good a job to turn down. Mrs. Adams wanted to do some shopping before they left to go to New York, so I went over at two-thirty in the afternoon to look after Craig.

Craig was feeling blue. Tuesday was his birthday and he had been given a nice lightweight nylon tent. Naturally he had wanted to use it right away. He wouldn't exactly admit it, but he was afraid to sleep outside in it by himself and had been hoping his father would spend the night with him. When he saw me I guess he figured I would make a good substitute.

"Want to go camping?" he asked. "I got a tent."

"Sure, I'll go camping with you sometime," I said.

As far as Craig was concerned, "sometime" meant that night. He began to make plans. At first he said he would pitch the tent beside the garage. Then he wanted to get farther from the house and to cook dinner out. Finally he had the bright idea we would go over and camp on the banks of the Delaware River. Mrs. Adams soon brought him down to earth.

"Henry is just going to be here until one o'clock or so," she said. "He doesn't want to sit out in the yard watching to see that you don't get scared of a rabbit or a cat or something."

"I wouldn't be scared of a rabbit or a cat," Craig said indignantly. "Why can't Henry sleep in the tent with me?"

"Maybe he doesn't want to sleep in a tent when he has a nice comfortable bed at home," Mrs. Adams said.

"I'd enjoy it," I told her. "And you wouldn't have to pay me for all night."

"Well, the weather is supposed to be good so I guess

there is no reason you can't," Mrs. Adams said after giving the matter some thought.

Immediately Craig began moving the tent farther and farther from the house. He didn't get to the Delaware this time, but he did manage to talk his mother into letting us go half a mile down the road to some woods owned by a Mr. Hendricks. We called Mr. Hendricks and got permission, and Mrs. Adams drove with us to see the exact spot where we planned to put the tent.

We went back to the Adams' home and got all our gear ready. I went home for my sleeping bag and some cooking utensils. By this time Mr. Adams was home and they changed clothes to go to New York. Mrs. Adams had packed some food for supper and breakfast, and had it ready in a box. They dropped us on their way. As the car disappeared down the road, Craig's face got longer and longer.

"New York is awful far away, isn't it?" he asked.

"Not so far. Your father and mother are going to drive in and be there in time for dinner."

"Does it get very dark here?" he asked.

"Not much darker than it does anywhere else," I said. "Of course there aren't any electric lights we can snap on, but we'll manage with a campfire and a flashlight."

"Do you think the spot back of the garage is better?"

If he had climbed a tree he could have seen the roof of his house, but I suppose it seemed a hundred miles away.

"Look, we can't go back now. Your parents may stop by on their way home to see how we are doing. If there's no tent and no sign of us they'll wonder what's happened. You wouldn't want to scare your mother silly, would you?"

"No," he said. "But I don't want to scare myself either."

"We've got to get moving," I said. "We've a lot of things to do."

I figured that the best thing to do was to keep him so busy that he wouldn't have time to worry or get homesick. For the next hour and a half I kept him hopping. First we carried our gear to our campsite and put up our tent. Then we began scouting around for stones for a fireplace. As soon as this was finished I put him to gathering firewood. I chopped and he carried. We worked for almost an hour and had much more firewood than we would ever need for cooking. However, I figured if he was really tired he'd sleep better and worry less. Also, if he got scared during the night, some extra wood for a fire would be handy.

By five-thirty he was not only tired, he was hungry. We started a fire and began cooking our dinner. Mrs. Adams believed in our camping in style. She had packed two steaks, a can of beans, a big package of potato chips, six rolls, some butter, a jar of pickles, some coleslaw, about a dozen brownies, a can of fruit, and a six-pack case of Cokes.

We built a sort of rock oven to warm the rolls, and we

heated the baked beans in a pan. Then, when the coals were just right, we broiled the steaks. Half the time when you are camping, the food is either burned or half cooked. But everything came out exactly right. I've never had a better steak. The only thing that was left when we finished were two rolls and a couple of brownies.

It was still light for more than an hour after we had finished eating, so we went for a walk along the stream. We had a fish pole with us so Craig tried fishing for a while. He caught one little minnow, which we tossed back. By this time it was getting dark and he began to get nervous. We went back to camp, threw a few sticks of wood on the fire, and turned in.

Craig was asleep almost as soon as he lay down. It was a mistake letting him go to sleep so early because he was rested enough by midnight to wake up.

"Henry, the fire's almost out," he said, shaking me.

After about six shakes I was finally awake enough to understand what he said.

"Let it go out," I said.

"But we're supposed to have a fire," he insisted.

"Not unless it's cold. Go back to sleep!"

"We need one to keep the wolves away," he said.

"Keep what wolves away?"

"There're wolves out there," he said in a scared voice. "I can hear them howling."

I listened and all I could hear was a dog barking way off

in the distance. It sounded a little like Agony. I'd considered bringing Agony along, but he yips at everything that makes a noise and I'd been afraid he'd keep us awake. As it was, he'd have been handy to chase away those wolves that Craig insisted he heard.

I got up and rebuilt our fire. Then I persuaded Craig to come outside where he could hear better. I'm not certain that I convinced him that there weren't any wolves, or whether the fire made him feel better. Anyhow, he finally relaxed and went back to sleep again.

At two o'clock he reached over and poked me again.

"There's some strange animal out there," he said. "A mountain lion, I bet."

"There's no mountain and no lions around here," I said. "It's probably a night bird of some kind."

I was about to drift off when he poked me again.

"There it was again! I heard it roaring!"

I listened for several minutes and then I heard *Garumph, garumph.*

"That's a frog," I told him. "A big bullfrog."

"Can frogs bite?" he asked in a worried voice.

"No, they don't bite, they don't scratch, and they don't kick people."

"Are they scared of a fire?" he asked.

I groaned and got to my feet. I stoked up the fire again, and once more he went to sleep. This time he slept until three-thirty.

"All right, I'll build the fire again," I said. "What do you think you heard this time?"

"I don't know, but it's awful," he said.

I had just stepped outside the tent when I heard it too. I was almost scared out of my wits. There was a hoot owl in a tree practically beside the tent, and he was in full voice. No matter how often you hear a hoot owl, it's always scary to hear that first hoot in the middle of the night.

"It's a hoot owl," I explained. "They won't hurt you and they're afraid of fire, so I'll put some wood on."

It was certainly lucky that I had had Craig gather so much wood. Even so, I used the last of it building a blaze to protect us from the owl. As soon as the fire was going, I tossed a few stones up into the tree and finally chased the owl away.

"If any more wild beasts start yowling, somebody is going to go out in the dark and gather wood before we can fix the fire," I said in a warning voice.

I guess that scared him, because nothing more happened until about five. I rolled over and a stick or something poked me in the back. I woke up enough to notice that it was quite light and that Craig was sound asleep. I drifted off again, positive that nothing more could happen. I was wrong.

"Hey, Henry. Someone is being killed!" Craig said half an hour later, shaking me. This time he was really scared.

"Who's being killed?" I asked.

"I don't know, but I heard him yelling for help. It was awful!"

I had an idea he had heard a rooster crowing somewhere, so I didn't pay much attention. Then suddenly I heard it too. There was a terrible scream of HELP! HELP! It sounded exactly as Craig said—as though someone were being murdered.

"What is it?" he asked.

"I don't know," I said. "Sounds like a woman screaming for help. And we ought to do something about it."

"What? What are you going to do, Henry?"

I didn't feel so good when I realized that I couldn't turn and ask somebody else the same question. I guess that's the way a captain of a ship feels when the ship is in danger and everyone expects him to do something. But, as Uncle Al said, I come from a long line of seagoing ancestors and I had to act as though I knew what I wanted to do even if I didn't.

"It sounded as though it came from that way," I said, pointing to the east. "We'll go find out what's happening."

"I don't want to go over there," Craig said. "I want to go home."

Home was in the opposite direction and that seemed like a good idea to me too. But if someone is screaming for help, you can't go off and leave them. None of the seagoing Harrises would have deserted someone who needed help.

"Let's go out to the road and head in that direction," I said. "We can make better time on the road."

We were almost to the road when we heard it again. It was a blood-curdling scream for help and it was repeated three times. Whoever was in trouble had enough strength left to do some powerful screaming. I felt less and less like going any closer, but when we reached the road we turned to the left toward the scream.

We hadn't gone very far before I saw a car coming toward us. I felt a lot better. When the car got closer I felt still better. It was the state police. I held up my hand to be certain it would stop.

"What are you two doing out so early?" the patrolman asked, rolling down his window.

"We've been camping, but we just heard a woman scream for help," I explained. "From that way, over there."

"Scream for help?" he asked doubtfully.

"Somebody was being killed," Craig said, his eyes almost as big as the car's headlights.

"I think you're imagining things, son," the patrolman said, smiling. "Maybe you heard an owl."

"It wasn't an owl," I said.

"No, it wasn't an owl," Craig agreed. "We heard owls and wolves last night."

"I see," the patrolman said. "Wolves, eh?" I could tell he didn't believe a word we were saying. He wasn't likely to unless I could keep Craig quiet for a few minutes and explain.

"There weren't wolves, but there *was* someone screaming for help. Just a few minutes ago."

I didn't have to say anything more because suddenly we heard the scream again. This time it was repeated twice. "Help! Help!"

"Jump in the car," the patrolman said. "We'll go see what the score is."

He had to turn around, which he did right there. "Where would you say that yell came from?" he asked.

"I'd say off there," I said, pointing.

We had gone only a short distance when we came to a lane in the woods.

"Where does that go?" he asked. "Anyone live on that lane?"

"I think there is a house back there. Anyhow it's in the right direction," I said.

"We'll try it," he said, turning the car into the lane.

We drove back into the woods about eight hundred yards and then the lane made a turn and suddenly we were out of the woods again and beside a house with several outbuildings.

It was a nice-looking one-story house with a double garage. There was a car in the garage and everything looked perfectly normal. Back of the house was a cinder-block barn or stable. There were several wooden outbuildings and three small fields fenced in with post-and-rail fence. Everything was neatly painted and very orderly. I could see some sheep in one pasture and a horse in another. There were some Muscovy ducks wandering around and some geese.

"It's not six o'clock yet and no one is going to appreciate crawling out of bed to answer questions, but I guess I'd better ask a few," the patrolman said, getting out of the car.

I got out the other side. Suddenly we heard the scream again. This time it was very close.

"Sounds as though it's over there behind that building," I said.

The patrolman thought so too and he started running toward the building. I followed, but I stayed well behind. After all he had a gun, and investigating calls for help was his job. Then the door of the house opened and a woman in a bathrobe came out.

"Don't pay any attention to that. That's Abernathy screaming."

"Who's Abernathy?" I asked.

"He's my pet peacock. All male peacocks scream like that. He doesn't do it often except at dusk and early in the morning. I usually keep him locked up but he wouldn't go in last night."

"I've never seen a peacock except in a zoo," I said. "Come on, Craig, let's go see the peacock."

Just as we rounded the corner of the building, the peacock stretched out his neck and gave a horrible scream for help. It almost split our eardrums.

"This is one they'll never believe back at headquarters," the patrolman said.

He was a beautiful peacock with his tail spread out like a fan. He strutted toward us and let out another scream. The officer looked at him, shook his head, and turned back toward his patrol car.

"Sorry to disturb you, lady, but that scream of his is enough to scare the wits out of anyone. Isn't there any way you can keep him from upsetting the neighborhood?"

"We're too far away from most houses for anyone to hear him," the woman said. "The few who can hear him know all about his screaming. And then, as I said, I try to keep him locked up."

We got back in the car and the patrolman took us back to where he had picked us up.

"I'm Patrolman Lenk," he said, holding out his hand. "All I can say is that if I'd been camping at this little lad's age and had heard anything like that, I'd have run in the other direction so fast no one could have caught up with me for a week."

It turned out Sergeant Lenk knew my Uncle Al. I invited him for breakfast, but he had already eaten. We went back, rebuilt our fire, and cooked bacon and eggs. A crow flew up in a tree nearby and began to complain.

"Are hawks afraid of fire?" Craig asked nervously.

"Don't worry about it," I said, not even bothering to tell him that it wasn't a hawk. "After that peacock, we can fight off any old hawks, eagles, or even condors that might come along."

Saturday, July 31st

While I was having all the trouble with little Belinda and her disappearing act, my Uncle Al said, "Henry, there are days that try men's souls. Now and then one comes along and you just have to grin and bear it." Today has been one of those days. Belinda was nothing compared to the trouble I had with things disappearing today.

I got a call this morning from a Mrs. Melick. She said Mrs. Wittenberg had recommended me and she wanted me to take care of their son Herman for the day while she and Mr. Melick went to Philadelphia. Herman, she explained, was between eight and nine and didn't need much looking after. However, they didn't want to go off and leave him alone. Since they were strangers in the area, he didn't have any friends where he could go and spend the day.

128

"We're visiting here for a few weeks," she explained. "We have a trailer parked beside my brother's house. It's on Berkley Road near the corner of Carver Lane. Do you know where that is?"

I did. It is about three miles from Uncle Al's, but the morning was cool and just right for a bicycle ride.

"Look for the name 'Nicholson' on the mailbox and a two-story shingle house painted dark red," she told me.

I found the place without any trouble. The trailer was parked at the edge of the driveway, a short distance from the house. The Nicholsons were both away but Mrs. Melick took me inside the trailer and showed me a key hanging on a hook.

"That's the key to the Nicholsons' back door in case you should need to go in the house and telephone," she said. "However, there should be everything you need here in the trailer."

There certainly was. Their trailer wasn't one of those huge things called "mobile homes" that they pull behind trucks, but a real trailer meant to be pulled behind a car. It was complete with everything. There was a kitchen with a gas stove that used bottled gas, a refrigerator, a bathroom, a generator to run the electric lights and the air-conditioning system. I learned later from Herman that his father was a construction engineer and he took the trailer all over the country. In summer Mrs. Melick and Herman went along.

"Here's the key to the trailer. In case you should go very far away, lock the door. Do you know where that dairy bar is near Lawrenceville?"

"Yes."

"Herman is anxious to take a bicycle ride. You see, he has never lived any place where there was any point in having a bicycle, and we certainly can't carry one around with us in the trailer. Do you think it would be safe to ride to that dairy bar for lunch?"

"We could get there and not take any main roads," I said, thinking about a strawberry soda.

"Fine! That solves the lunch question. The bike belongs to Herman's cousin, who outgrew it years ago. However, it's not ours so see that he takes good care of it."

She gave me money for lunch for both of us, warning me not to give Herman any or he would lose it. Otherwise she didn't give me a mess of instructions the way some parents do. She left things to my good judgment, but then, of course, the Henry Reed Baby-Sitting Service has a reputation for being on the ball. At least it did have until today.

Herman was all right, but very quiet and sort of dull—I couldn't find much to interest him. We fooled around the back yard for a while, and then he wanted to go for a ride on his bike. I locked the trailer and we started up the road. I took a roundabout way and slowly headed for the dairy bar. We went almost two extra miles and still got there about eleven-thirty. We were both hungry so we decided to go ahead and eat lunch. There were only four cars, all near the door, but I carefully took our bikes over to the far side of the parking lot and parked them in the grass.

There were practically no customers inside so we had our choice of seats at the counter. I ordered a strawberry soda, a hamburger with everything, and an order of French fries. Herman had the same, except that he ordered a chocolate milk shake.

The milk shake and soda were ready first and the waitress started to bring them. She was carrying the soda and an empty glass in one hand and the chocolate milk shake in a metal mixing container. The edge of the rubber floor mat was turned up and she tripped just before she got to us. She dropped the soda and the empty glass. The metal container of milk shake slipped out of her hand, hit the edge of the counter, and then took to the air. Herman was wearing a white T shirt, but in less than a second it was covered with brown polka dots. But what he got was only a taste. Most of it hit me. I was wearing a sport shirt and shorts and both were soaked.

When you get your mouth all set for a delicious strawberry soda and instead you get a chocolate milk shake in your lap, it's a shock. It's no fun having cold ice cream go down your neck or all over your bare legs. Besides, I don't like chocolate.

The waitress was almost as upset as I was. The manager came hurrying over and took us back to the washroom. He apologized and did his best to get us cleaned up. We finally got most of the chocolate washed off, but we felt sticky all over.

The place had filled up while we were in the washroom, but the waitress had saved our seats. The manager told us we could have anything we wanted free so we both ordered two hamburgers this time. While we were waiting I looked across the room and saw Johnny Sebastian sitting with some boy I didn't know. He had his mouth full of hamburger and was busy stuffing it with more.

We were really hungry by this time and the strawberry soda was almost worth the trouble we'd had. Just as we were finishing, Johnny Sebastian and his friend got up to leave. He saw me as he was paying the cashier and waved. We were ready to go, but I waited because I didn't want him to see me looking like a chocolate milk shake. He would have made all sorts of silly remarks.

Since we didn't have to pay, we were only a minute behind Johnny. As we stepped outside, he backed out of the parking space with a roar, went halfway across the parking lot in reverse, whammed into our bikes with his rear bumper, and knocked them down. He didn't even look back but slammed the car into first gear and went roaring off. I suppose it could have been accidental. I don't know how he could have known one of the bikes was mine and possibly he didn't know he hit them. Still, that MG had done it again. Herman's bike wasn't damaged, but mine fell against his and bent a fender support somehow. I had to straighten it before I could ride and even then the fender rubbed a little.

Herman seemed to be a little bit more alive on the way back. Maybe all he needed was something to eat, although he was a pudgy boy who didn't look underfed. On our way back we saw several butterflies, and at first he wouldn't believe me when I explained that they were caterpillars before they were butterflies. I've always liked natural history and my mother has taught me a lot about insects. Herman didn't know anything, but he was interested. We took our time pedaling back, talking about different things we saw along the way.

"There's some Cokes in the refrigerator," Herman said as we turned into the Nicholson driveway. "Let's have one."

"Good idea," I said, reaching into my pocket for the key. I found the key and turned toward the trailer. It wasn't there. I looked around, wondering what was wrong.

"Are we in the right place?" I asked.

"Somebody took our trailer!" Herman said, looking as though he were about to cry.

I could understand how he felt. After all, he lived in that trailer and to find it gone was like coming home and finding somebody had jacked up your house and moved it away. I wasn't feeling very good about it either. A baby-sitter is hired mainly to look after the baby, but he isn't supposed to let the house be stolen out from under him either.

"You don't suppose your mother and father could have come back and taken it, do you?" I asked.

"And left me?" Herman asked, his lower lip trembling.

"No, I guess not," I said.

I had to do something, and the only thing I could think of was to call my Uncle Al for advice. Since it was Saturday, I knew he would be home. The trouble was that the key to the house was in the trailer. I walked around the house with Herman. Every window had a screen on it and the screens were fastened. The windows were probably locked too; I couldn't tell. I didn't feel like going to the neighbors and having them listen while I explained my trouble, so we went around the house again. This time I spotted a window without a screen above the back porch. Very often second floor windows have no locks.

"Is there a ladder in the garage?" I asked Herman.

"I don't know," he said. "But if you could climb that tree you wouldn't need one."

He was right. It was a simple matter to climb the maple right beside the porch and step over onto the porch roof. For once something went well and the window opened with very little trouble. I made my way downstairs and found the telephone. I dialed Uncle Al's number, but the line was busy.

I tried three times and then decided to call the state police. I had a feeling that that was what Uncle Al would advise me to do anyhow.

"State police, Sergeant Lenk speaking," a voice said promptly.

"This is Henry Reed, Sergeant Lenk," I said.

"How are you, Henry? Want to report somebody's being murdered again?"

"No, sir," I said. "I want to report a lost trailer."

"What kind of a trailer?" he asked. "That one your uncle pulls with his little garden tractor?"

"No, a house trailer."

"I see," he said with a chuckle. "Just what were you doing with a house trailer that you should lose it?"

"I didn't exactly lose it," I said. "It simply disappeared."

"Henry, you just don't go around losing house trailers and they don't disappear into thin air. Now what are you trying to pull?"

"This really happened," I insisted. "I'm baby-sitting with a boy called Herman Melick. His father and mother went to Philadelphia. We went to get something to eat at the dairy bar and someone stole his house trailer."

"Where are you calling from?" Sergeant Lenk asked.

135

"From the Nicholsons' on Berkley Road near Carver Lane."

"Let me speak to Mr. or Mrs. Nicholson," Lenk asked.

"They're away for a few days," I explained.

"This better not be another case of a peacock yelling for help," Sergeant Lenk said, sounding very doubtful. "I've got to stay here for a few minutes, but then I'll be over to investigate. And if I find that trailer hidden under a bush, I'll throw you in jail."

I tried Uncle Al again twice but the telephone was still busy. My Aunt Mabel doesn't talk much on the telephone but she has some friends that have an awful lot to say. Finally I gave up and called Midge.

I can't understand Midge at times. She seemed to think it was a big joke that the trailer had disappeared.

"Cool!" she said. "You're part of a famous crime, Henry. It's like the great train robbery in England. Imagine how it will look in the paper—someone steals an entire house and everything in it. It's probably insured and Mrs. Melick can go out and buy all new clothes! Just think of that!"

"And just think that when they get home tonight they won't have any place to sleep."

"They'll find some place. The Red Cross will do something, or maybe the President will call this a disaster area. He might fly over in a helicopter."

"Be serious," I told her. "I feel sort of responsible."

"It wasn't your fault," Midge said. "She told you to go to the dairy bar."

"Will you go see Uncle Al or Aunt Mabel and tell them about this?" I asked. "The phone seems to be busy. Tell them I may want to bring Herman home for the night."

"I can see your uncle from here," Midge said. "He's working in the yard. We're about to leave for Princeton and I'll ask Mom to stop on the way."

"If you're going to Princeton, tell the Princeton police about it," I suggested. "Maybe they saw it go through."

"Don't be silly," Midge said. "The Princeton police never look for anything except parking meters that have expired. What did the trailer look like?"

The trailer looked like most other shiny aluminum trailers except that it had a narrow red band around the upper part and of course it had a California license. I described it to Midge and said good-by. I had expected to be able to open the house door from the inside, but none of the three doors had the spring-type lock that you can open without a key. There was nothing I could do but leave the way I had come.

I had started down the trunk of the tree when my pants caught on one of the metal brackets that hold the gutter along the edge of the porch roof. There I was with my arms wrapped around the tree and caught by the seat of my pants. I wasn't in much danger. If I had dropped all the way to the ground it wouldn't have hurt me. The only trouble was that there wouldn't be much left of my pants.

"What's the matter?" Herman asked.

"My pants are caught on that bracket," I said. "I guess I'll have to climb up and get loose."

I planned to climb up far enough to pull my shorts loose, but I got only about three inches. I was hooked and couldn't move either way. The trunk was smooth and I needed both hands to hold on.

"See if there is a ladder in the garage," I told Herman. "I need something to stand on so I can use at least one of my hands."

He ran to the garage and came back in less than a minute. There was a ladder but it was too heavy for him to lift.

"I'll get somebody to help," he said.

Before I could stop him he had disappeared down the driveway. I had no idea where he went or how long he would be gone. The nearest neighbor was some distance up the road. I didn't like the idea at all. He might go running along the road and be hit by a car and the baby-sitter who was supposed to look after him would be up a tree, caught by the seat of his pants. I called after him, but he either didn't hear or didn't pay any attention.

I squeezed real tight with my legs and one arm and managed to get my right hand around my back. I was trying to work the cloth loose from the bracket when I heard Herman again.

138

"I stopped a car. There's a man coming."

I looked down and there was Mr. Sylvester. He's the editor of the *Princeton Bugle,* and if there was anyone I didn't want to see at that point it was a newspaper man. Mr. Sylvester likes to write what he thinks are humorous articles, and I didn't care to have one written about my being caught up in a tree. Even if he just stuck to the facts, it wouldn't sound very good for a baby-sitter to be in such a silly fix while the kid he was supposed to be looking after went to the rescue.

"Well, well, if it isn't my old friend Henry Reed," Mr. Sylvester said. "You seem to be out on a limb. Figuratively speaking, of course, because that seems to be the main trunk you're clinging to. What are you trying to do?"

"I was trying to telephone someone," I said. "Herman, show him where the ladder is."

"That's a rather odd answer; I don't see any telephone up there," Mr. Sylvester said. "Still, I suppose the important thing is to get you down. We can get the facts later. Pity I don't have a camera."

I was glad he didn't have because my picture would have been in that week's *Princeton Bugle* for certain— probably a rear view too.

He got the ladder and put it up against the edge of the porch. Once I had something to stand on and could use my hands, it didn't take long to get free. I climbed down and Mr. Sylvester and I put the ladder away.

"I'm interested in knowing why you climbed a tree to telephone," Mr. Sylvester said.

"The Nicholsons, who live here, are Herman's aunt and uncle," I explained. "They're away and the house is locked. I had to telephone so I climbed up on the back porch and went in through the window."

"I suppose that's logical enough if one is agile enough to climb a tree," Mr. Sylvester said. "I don't have much of a story though, because I can't very well say in the paper that one can get in the house through the rear window over the porch. It would encourage burglars."

"There really isn't much to it," I said, feeling better now that I was down with my pants in one piece and Mr. Sylvester was acting so sensible.

"We wouldn't have had to climb the tree, but someone stole the key," Herman said.

I looked at him and shook my head, but he didn't see me. Besides I think it was too late. Mr. Sylvester can smell a story a mile away.

"Who stole the key?" Mr. Sylvester asked.

"I don't know," Herman said. "It was in our trailer and when they took that they took the key too."

"Do you mean someone took your trailer? When?"

"About noon," I said. "We went to the dairy bar for lunch and when we got back the trailer had disappeared. The reason I wanted to get to the telephone was to call the police."

"I don't have any place to live any more," Herman said mournfully.

Mr. Sylvester got out his notebook and pencil and began taking notes. He finally got through asking questions and went back to his car. He had been gone only a minute or two when Uncle Al drove up the driveway. He got out and I had to explain it all to him.

"Do you and Herman want to come back home with me now?" he asked.

"The Melicks won't know what's happened if I do that," I objected. "They'll come home and find no home and no Herman either."

"I could bring you back about five-thirty," Uncle Al said. "You say they're not due back until about six. Of course, it's a nice day and there's no reason why you can't stay here if you want."

We hadn't decided what to do when a state police car stopped out front. Sergeant Lenk got out and I had to go over the whole story again.

He walked to the front of the place and tried to find tire tracks to learn which way the trailer had turned. There wasn't much to be seen. If there had been any marks Uncle Al's car had covered them when it came in the lane. We were all standing by the road talking, when the Glasses' car appeared. Midge jumped out.

"You can all put away your guns!" she announced. "The criminals have been caught. Just call me Sherlock Glass!"

"What do you mean?" I asked.

"I've cracked the case," she said proudly. "On second thought, I think I'll call myself Midge Bond, secret agent, 08525. That's my zip-code number."

When she finally got around to talking sense, she told us that on their way to Princeton they had passed a pickup truck pulling a trailer. The trailer answered my description so they stopped at the next house and called the state police.

"I must have just left," Lenk said. "I wonder if they've caught up with it yet. I'd better call in."

He went back to the police car to use the radio. He was still talking when a pickup truck appeared, pulling a trailer. Behind it was a second police car.

"Jimmy's Service Station," Uncle Al said, looking at the truck. "I suspect all this excitement has been a mistake."

He was right. Jimmy was supposed to pick up a trailer about a mile away to align the wheels. His driver got the directions mixed and picked up the wrong trailer. It had never occurred to him that there might be two trailers almost alike within a mile of each other.

No one had realized the mistake until the owner of the other trailer had called to find out why Jimmy hadn't appeared as he had promised. The trailer was on its way back when Midge saw it.

"Tell your dad he got a free wheel-alignment job," Jimmy said. "It needed it too. That right wheel was canted in too much and was wearing the tire on the inside."

"I guess there's no harm done," Sergeant Lenk said.

They parked the trailer in the same spot and everyone left. Herman and I got two Cokes from the refrigerator and drank them. He decided to take a nap. I stretched out on the sofa and did the same thing.

Saturday, August 7th

It's been a good week. We've been fairly busy, but not rushed—which is just as well. Too much baby-sitting can be just like too much of anything—tiresome. We were busy Monday and Tuesday and part of Wednesday, but Thursday we had no jobs at all. Uncle Al took the day off and he and Aunt Mabel took Midge and me to the beach.

Mr. Sylvester's story about the missing house trailer appeared in the *Princeton Bugle*, but it didn't say much about me. It told how Jimmy's Service Station got mixed up and was sort of funny. I don't believe the publicity has hurt the Henry Reed Baby-Sitting Service.

Belinda hasn't tried her disappearing act all week. I think she's cured. Midge took the morning shift both Monday and Tuesday, and I took the afternoons. Monday afternoon a Mrs. Sansome arrived with twins, a boy and a girl named Timothy and Dorothy. They had been invited over to the Osborns' to play with Belinda. It's almost as easy to watch three as one, so I didn't mind—especially when Mrs. Sansome gave me an extra dollar.

The three children played fairly peacefully with one another. I had to settle a couple of arguments, but otherwise I didn't have much to do except to watch them while they were in the pool. All three are good swimmers so it was an easy afternoon.

We were all lying beside the pool sunning ourselves and I was half asleep when I heard Belinda say, "My daddy collects stamps. He has a great big book and he sticks stamps in it."

"My daddy collects money," Dorothy said.

I thought that she meant that he collected old coins as many people do. Usually they specialize in nickels, or pennies, or some particular coin.

"What kind of money does he collect?" I asked.

"All kinds," Timmy said. "He collects taxes."

"Does he work for the government?" I asked.

"The Internal—Internal something," Timmy said.

"The Internal Revenue Service?"

"Yes, I think that's it, and he's being transferred. We're going to move to Philadelphia."

I figured the Sansomes were good people to stay away from and that the sooner they moved to Philadelphia the more relaxed the Grover's Corner area would be. I started

146

to ask Timmy if his father had had anything to do with my getting all those income tax forms, but decided it was smarter to keep quiet.

Mrs. Osborn was fifteen minutes late and it was six forty-five by the time I got home. Aunt Mabel was just putting the dinner on the table.

"A man was here five minutes ago looking for you," Uncle Al said. "I was outside working on the azaleas." He paused and fished in his pocket and came up with a crumpled slip of paper. "Wrote his name down and asked if you'd call him."

I looked at the slip of paper. The name was Lionel Sansome. After dinner I looked in the telephone book and there was only one Sansome. He had to be Timmy's and Dorothy's father. I certainly wasn't anxious to call an internal revenue agent. Since he hadn't said when to call, I decided the matter could wait until a day or two before I leave this fall.

Tuesday afternoon I was at the Osborns again, taking care of Belinda. About five minutes of six a strange car drove in and a tall man with a bald head began walking across the lawn.

"That's Dorothy's daddy," Belinda said.

I didn't want to see Dorothy's daddy but there wasn't any place I could hide.

"Are you Henry Reed, President of the Henry Reed Baby-Sitting Service?" he asked.

147

He was smiling in a friendly enough way, but I thought he might be trying to trap me. Even though Uncle Al had said I didn't owe any tax, I didn't think it would be wise to do any boasting about how well our firm was doing.

"That's right," I said. "It really is just Midge Glass and myself. We're not a big firm."

"Well, all I need is one responsible baby-sitter for Friday. Are you free?"

"Yes, sir!" I said. I felt sort of guilty about not calling him the night before, now that I knew that all he wanted was a baby-sitter.

"If you could be at our house about eleven A.M. on Friday, I'd appreciate it," he said. "Mrs. Sansome and I are going house-hunting in Philadelphia. I arranged some time ago at the office to take the day off. I set up several appointments with a real-estate agent. Now it turns out that a very good prospect for my house here can't come any time except tomorrow afternoon. What I really want is a house-sitter as much as a baby-sitter."

Mrs. Osborn came home while we were talking, so we put my bike in the back of Mr. Sansome's station wagon and I went home with him. He showed me how the sump pump operated, pointed out that the house had a new roof and aluminum storm windows, and showed me the boundaries of their grounds.

"This man is from the city," he warned me. "His name is Kirby and he's being transferred east from Cleveland. I think my house is the right size and about the right price for him. The only hitch is that he may think this is too far out in the country and too lonesome."

Mr. Sansome's house was an attractive two-story house about fifteen years old. It was surrounded by half a dozen other houses in a little settlement like Grover's Corner. I didn't see how anyone could feel he was too far in the country with all those houses, and I told Mr. Sansome that.

"You can't, but you're used to Grover's Corner," he said. "To some people, any place that doesn't have street lights and a drugstore in the next block is real frontier country."

Mr. Sansome drove me home. He was very easy to talk to and seemed like a good egg. Finally I got up nerve and asked him about the forms I had received. He asked me a few questions and then told me to pay no attention to them, it had all been a mistake.

"With forms going out to about a hundred million people and I don't know how many million companies, it's a wonder the wrong forms don't get sent to the wrong place more often."

"That was the income tax collector," I said to Uncle Al as I walked into the house. "I've got a baby-sitting job to do for him."

"Now that's a switch," Uncle Al said, looking up from his paper. "I'm proud of you, Henry. You're the only member of our family who was ever able to reverse the

149

process and get money from the internal revenue collector. Was this the man who wanted to see you last night?"

"That's right—Mr. Sansome. The Sansomes live over in that little group of houses on Federal Road. They have twins."

"Think of that," Uncle Al said. "An internal revenue man who is practically a neighbor of mine. He's married and has children. Just a normal citizen with the usual collection of problems."

"Why shouldn't he be?" Aunt Mabel asked.

"Just throws a man off base," Uncle Al complained. "He should have horns or something. Be careful, Henry. It may be a trap. He's probably a secret agent."

Uncle Al does a lot of kidding and I'm never absolutely certain when he is and when he isn't. When I went over to the Sansomes' on Friday I kept my eyes open. It didn't take me long to decide that at least Mrs. Sansome wasn't any secret agent. If there was ever anyone who was a normal citizen with the usual collection of problems, it was her.

She had done a big wash that morning and was taking it off the line. As I appeared she folded the last piece and put it in the basket. She looked tired and worried and nervous. I carried the basket in for her and put it on a little table on the screened-in back porch.

"I don't have any lunch made yet, I haven't changed

clothes, and I'm supposed to meet Lionel in Trenton in ten minutes," she said. "What a morning! A washing to do, the house to clean, three telephone calls, an insurance agent and a real-estate man to look at the house."

"I can fix lunch if you'll tell me what you want the twins to have."

"There's some luncheon meat in the refrigerator. Make them some sandwiches and have them eat outside. In fact, keep them outside as much as possible. I'd like the house to look orderly and neat when the Kirbys look at it tonight."

"When will they be here?"

"Sometime after four." She opened the refrigerator and pointed to the meat drawer. "There are some wieners and some hamburgers. If you don't mind, build a fire out in the grill and cook whichever you want for dinner tonight. We won't be home until later. There's a bowl of salad, and potato chips in that cupboard. There are Cokes and milk. And don't let them tell you they don't have to drink their milk."

Mrs. Sansome rushed upstairs and in less than five minutes had changed. She put bobby pins in her hair on the way to the car and part way out the drive she stopped suddenly and rolled down the window.

"Henry, would you be kind enough to take the hose and soak that bed of marigolds and zinnias beside the step? They look sort of wilted."

She must have looked in the mirror because she sat with the motor running and put on some lipstick. Then she called out, "And above all, don't let the cat in the house! He sheds long hair all over."

The twins played in the back yard while I watered the bed of flowers. I had just finished and was coiling up the hose when a big Persian cat came walking across the lawn. He went over and began smelling the flowers.

"That's Shakespeare," Dorothy said. "He's the one Mommy said to keep out of the house."

The telephone rang and I went inside to answer it. It was Mr. Kirby. He explained that he had been held up and might not get there until about five-thirty. I said that would be all right and started back outside. I opened the screen door to step out when a red MG came roaring in the drive. It wasn't coming so terribly fast but it was making a lot of noise. As it reached the end of the drive, the driver slammed on the brakes and gave a blast on his horn. Of course it was Johnny Sebastian.

The cat had disappeared while I was on the telephone, but evidently he had been hiding behind the zinnias or smelling them or just wandering through the flower bed. The roar of the MG and the blast on the horn scared him and triggered him into action. He came out of the flower bed like a flash. He raced up the steps, rushed in between my legs and through the half-open screen door. While I turned to yell at him, he shot across the porch, leaped into the air, and landed square in the middle of the basket of clean clothes. He arched his back and began to snarl and spit.

I couldn't decide whether to tell Johnny Sebastian what I thought of his coming in a driveway that way, or to try to get Shakespeare out of the house. I picked the cat first. I moved toward him and he backed across the basket, stomping his big muddy feet on any clothes he had missed before. Then, when I was about to grab him, he gave a leap and raced into the kitchen.

His feet were a mess from the wet flower bed. From the number of tracks he made on the kitchen linoleum you would have thought he was a centipede. I finally caught him in the upstairs bathroom. I took him outside and went back to survey the damage.

The kitchen floor was all spotted, but that wasn't too difficult to repair. Dorothy showed me where the mop was kept and I soon had the floor looking decent again. Then I followed Shakespeare's path upstairs, cleaning up as I went. Finally I got around to looking at the laundry. How Mrs. Sansome had folded it, I can't imagine, but somehow she managed to get at least half the clothes on the top layer and the cat had left muddy footprints on every piece.

"Mommy is going to be mad when she gets home," Dorothy said, looking at one of Timmy's T shirts. "She hates to do the wash."

"I'm mad right now," I said. "What did that crazy Johnny Sebastian want?"

"He had the wrong house," Tim said. "He wanted Dick Mayhew. He lives next door."

I couldn't think of anything to do with the muddy clothes except to wash them again. Dorothy found the soap powder and I was able to figure out how to operate the automatic washer. After the wash was started, I got lunch. We had ham-and-cheese sandwiches, which we ate outside. Johnny Sebastian's car was parked next door in the driveway, but he was out of sight somewhere.

I thought about that car while I was eating. I am beginning to agree with Midge. There's something mean about that MG. It's got a character of its own. It makes more noise and has a more annoying horn than other MGs of the same model. An ordinary car wouldn't have scared that cat, and I wouldn't have had all that extra work.

The laundry was finished by the time we had eaten lunch. I looked around for a dryer but there wasn't one. I guess Mrs. Sansome is one of those people who believe fresh air and sunshine make the wash smell better. I started outside but I saw Johnny and his friend in the back yard, practicing putting. If I hung out the wash Johnny Sebastian would notice and make all sorts of remarks about my being a washwoman. I didn't mind doing the washing. I just didn't want Johnny to catch me at it. I

154

put the basket by the porch door and went outside with the twins.

"Aren't you going to hang up the wash?" Dorothy asked. "It's all wet."

"We'll hang it after a while."

Three little neighbor boys came over a short while later and we had a baseball game of sorts. While we were playing, Johnny Sebastian and his friend got in the car and drove away. I had forgotten about the wash, but after the game was over Dorothy went into the house for something and noticed it.

"Aren't you going to hang up the wash?" she asked. "It's still all wet."

I picked up the basket and started down the steps when the MG roared in the Mayhews' lane again. I put the basket back on the porch.

"Aren't you going to hang up the clothes?" Dorothy asked again. She is going to be a real worrier when she grows up and has something to worry about.

"Not right now," I said. "That MG causes trouble. It will knock down the clothesline or do something; I know from experience."

Before I knew it, it was almost six o'clock. I hadn't noticed but Johnny Sebastian had disappeared again. The Kirbys still hadn't arrived to look at the house but I decided I'd better get started with dinner anyhow. The

Sansomes have a very fancy grill in the back yard. There were part of a bag of charcoal briquets and some kindling, so in a few minutes I had a fire going. We brought out the salad and other things while the fire was burning down. It was almost ready and I was about to go for the hamburgers and wieners when a man appeared from next door.

"Hello, I'm Harvey Simpson," he said, holding out his hand. "I live next door. Lionel around?"

"I'm Henry Reed," I told him. "I'm baby-sitting for the Sansomes. They went to Philadelphia."

"I came over to borrow some charcoal. You can tell Lionel I'll get him a new bag tomorrow."

"I used the last there was for this fire," I said.

"Well, I should have bought some on my way home," he said.

"Why don't you cook on this fire? There's lots of room and these briquets will last for hours."

"That's a good idea," he said. "You're a lifesaver."

He was gone several minutes and then reappeared with four steaks. I put them on the grill and told Dorothy to go inside and get our hamburgers and hot dogs.

"I didn't bring a fork," Mr. Simpson said. "Watch those for a minute, will you?"

He left again, but this time he didn't come back. I seared the steaks and then moved them away from the hottest part of the fire so they wouldn't be cooked too fast.

Finally I sent Timmy over to tell him that they would be done shortly. Four people came back with Tim, Mr. and Mrs. Simpson, and two friends.

"I'm sorry, Henry," Mr. Simpson said. "As I walked into the house the telephone rang and it was a long-distance call. I've been all this time on the telephone."

"And we were in the other room and didn't even realize the steaks were on," Mrs. Simpson said. She had brought a tray with the rest of their dinner, which she put on the picnic table. She came over to look at the steaks.

"Umm, they look wonderful," she said. "Much better than when Harvey does them."

Dorothy appeared with a package of wieners and hamburgers. "Aren't you going to hang out the wash, Henry?" she asked. "It's still all wet."

"What wash, Dorothy?" Mrs. Simpson asked.

"The cat walked through the mud and then jumped on Mrs. Sansome's wash," I explained. "I did it over, but I forgot to hang it out." I turned to Dorothy. "We'll hang it right now, before we cook our dinner."

"You cooked our steaks, we'll hang your wash," Mrs. Simpson said. "We'll have just enough time."

Mrs. Simpson got the basket and the clothespins and all four of them began hanging wash on the line. It was quite a scene—two men and two women hanging up pants and undershirts, me cooking dinner, and the twins running around and getting in the way. Right in the middle of it all Johnny Sebastian drove in the Mayhews' drive again to bring Dick Mayhew home. He looked across at all the activity and I could see he was puzzled. I looked inscrutable the way a secret agent does in the movies.

To add to the confusion, a couple appeared and announced that they were the Kirbys. I had put the hamburgers and hot dogs on by this time and the steaks were ready to take off except for one that Mrs. Simpson wanted well done. I couldn't very well leave.

"I'm sorry to interrupt everything," Mr. Kirby said. "I got tied up in traffic coming out of New York, and then I had trouble with my radiator."

"Have you had anything to eat?" Mr. Simpson asked, after everybody had been introduced.

They hadn't. Both the twins wanted hot dogs, so I had plenty of hamburger. I put some on for them. Everybody sat down at the picnic table. We ate in installments since different things were ready at different times, but we had a good time. We used paper plates so there wasn't much cleaning up to do. What there was, the Simpsons did while I showed the Kirbys through the house.

"Seems like a very friendly neighborhood," Mr. Kirby said. "We were afraid it would be sort of dull out here in the country."

"Don't worry about that," I said. "Something happens

every minute. As the leading baby-sitter in the area, I know. It's never dull!"

Mr. Sansome called me this morning. The Kirbys have decided to buy the house. Mr. Sansome was very pleased.

"You did a fine job, Henry." he said. "The Kirbys were impressed with how friendly everyone was. I don't suppose we'll be able to send you much baby-sitting business since we're moving away, but if I can ever do you a favor let me know."

I told Uncle Al later that if he ever has any trouble with the Internal Revenue Department to let me know. I've got influence there.

Sunday, August 15th

This has been a big week in the history of the Henry Reed Baby-Sitting organization. We have expanded. Uncle Al says that we have to be careful or the Justice Department will sue us for having a monopoly. I don't think we'll be sued, but we have about cornered the baby-sitting market in the Grover's Corner area.

The idea was mostly Midge's. We've had Mondays and Tuesdays booked for some time to take care of Belinda. Last Sunday two other people called and wanted us to baby-sit on Tuesday. Of course you can't baby-sit in three places at one time.

"We ought to start a nursery school and take in all the tots in the countryside," Midge suggested.

It was a brilliant idea because there is the empty barn

sitting on my mother's lot. It has a good roof and there is a nice grassy area that is just right for a playground.

"We can make sandwiches at your house or mine and take them over to the barn," Midge suggested. "And if they want to use the bathroom, they can use our house."

"We need furniture," I reminded her. "They can't sit on the floor; it's dirty. I don't want to wash any more clothes."

"Furniture is the easiest part of all," Midge said. "Everyone has old furniture. We have a sofa and a chair in our garage for a starter."

Midge was right. In less than two hours we had a table, an old desk, and three straight chairs, in addition to the sofa and the easy chair. We spent most of Sunday afternoon sweeping out the barn, washing the windows, and collecting the furniture. We used Uncle Al's garden tractor and cart and soon had everything at the barn. Agony was very excited by the whole operation. He has missed me this summer; I've been away on business so much.

It was about four in the afternoon when we finally had the place in some sort of order. Midge collapsed on the sofa and looked around at everything.

"Cozy," she said. "Very cozy. We've got one problem though. How do we get our clients here?"

"The parents have to deliver them. We can offer some sort of inducement."

"Some sort of what?" Midge asked.

"Inducement. We might give them one hour of free baby-sitting, for example."

"I'm no genius at math, but that won't work," Midge said. "If some mother brought her child for only half an hour and we promised her an hour of baby-sitting for nothing, we'd owe her thirty-seven and a half cents."

We decided to supply the lunch in return for the mother's bringing the child. We picked Tuesday to start our new operation. Midge called the two people who had wanted baby-sitters. One had found someone, but the other one was happy with the arrangement and so was Mrs. Osborn.

Wednesday was slow with only one customer. Thursday and Friday we had three, and Saturday we hit the jackpot with five most of the day.

Of course nothing ever runs perfectly smoothly, even a well-organized business like ours. Midge had a little difficulty Saturday morning, but we soon took care of the trouble.

After all five of our group had arrived and Midge had them busy in a game of softball, I went home to mow the lawn. At eleven I went back with a pitcher of lemonade. They were all playing outside but there was something odd about the way they acted. Midge motioned for me to follow her toward the barn.

"There's something peculiar going on," she said in a low

voice when we were far enough away to talk. "We were all playing out there and little Barbara Benham went inside the barn for something. She came running out a minute later, scared silly. She insisted she heard someone moaning in there. I went in but couldn't hear a thing. I even went up in the loft. There was nothing there except two pigeons."

"Do you suppose she's making it up?"

"I thought so for a while. Then Danny Wittenberg claimed there was something wrong with the bat, so I sent him over to get the other one. He came dashing out saying that there was a ghost inside. Now they're all acting like a bunch of silly sheep. None of them wants to go near the barn."

It was my turn to furnish the lunch so I went home to make it. I brought it back and Midge and I served it in the barn. They didn't like the idea much, but they were hungry. All of us ate inside and we didn't hear a sound. We ran out of milk and Midge ran over to her house for some more. While she was gone I went outside and left the five children in the barn by themselves. Nothing happened, and I thought the whole matter had been settled.

It was my turn to take charge during the afternoon while Midge went home to do some work for her mother. About one o'clock a little girl named Ellen decided to finish her sandwich, which she had wrapped in waxed paper and left in the barn. She didn't want to go in alone and neither Barbara nor the other little girl would go in with her.

"You go over with her, Danny," I said. "Prove you're not scared of anything in that barn."

He finally let me persuade him. They had just gone inside when they came dashing back out again, their eyes big as soup plates.

"Somebody's dying in there," Danny insisted. "I heard him."

There wasn't much doubt that they had heard something. I walked over to the barn, climbed up to the second floor, or loft, and looked there. There wasn't anything that could have moaned.

I took Danny to the edge of the road to make certain that no cars were coming, and then sent him across the street for Midge. When she arrived I told her what had happened.

"They're hearing something, there's no question about that. You pretend that you are taking charge again and I'll start home. Then I'll sneak back and go in the barn through that window on the other side. When I'm inside you send someone over after something."

"No one will go," Midge objected.

"Danny will if he knows I am already inside."

Danny didn't like the idea, but he finally agreed.

I waved good-by and walked down the road toward

Aunt Mabel's. Then I slipped into the trees and sneaked back on the opposite side of the barn. I made a little noise opening the window, but I got inside without much trouble. I sat down on the floor beside the big chair and waited quietly.

I guess Danny had a change of heart after I left because he had two others with him when he arrived. The three had barely stepped inside when there was a blood-chilling moan.

"Save me, save me!" a mournful voice said. Then there was another moan.

The three children didn't wait after the first moan, and if I had been them I wouldn't have either. In fact I was scared myself for a minute. But the moan seemed to come from the rafters and I had an idea what it was. The light in the barn isn't too good and the first time I looked, I didn't find anything. But on the second inspection I found a small speaker. It had been wedged in a corner where one of the big beams meets the wall stud. I moved the table over to stand on. A black double wire led away from the speaker, along the ceiling, and finally out through a knothole near the back of the barn.

I went near enough to the door to motion to Midge. The kids were all standing around her and you could see that this last scare hadn't made them any happier. I waited inside, out of sight, until Midge arrived.

"Somebody has a speaker up by that rafter," I told her.

"The wire goes out that corner. There's a microphone on the other end, I suppose. Whoever it is must be able to see what we're doing out there. He scares the kids when they're alone, but he doesn't make a sound when we're along."

"Johnny Sebastian!" Midge said in a rage.

"If it is Johnny he must be out back in the woods. He couldn't see what was going on from his place because of the hedge."

"That rat!" Midge said. "I'm going out and give him a piece of my mind. Scaring little kids! The big bully!"

I thought it was a pretty clever rig myself, but of course I didn't want our baby-sitting business ruined, the way he was fast doing it.

"We've got to prove it is Johnny," I said.

"I've got proof. He's the only one in Grover's Corner low enough to do it!"

"That's just circumstantial evidence," I said. "We need proof. The thing to do is to put on some sort of an act as though everyone is unhappy over here. Take them over to your house. Maybe your mother will look after them for a few minutes. Go down the road and come up on the other side of the barn the way I did. I'll slip out of the window and wait for you. Then we'll follow the wire. Maybe we'll catch him red-handed."

"All right," Midge agreed. She picked up the little hatchet we keep in the barn for chopping up firewood.

166

"I'm going to take this along and when I come to some place where I can reach the wire I'm going to chop it in about six pieces."

She left the barn carrying the hatchet. A short distance outside she turned and put one hand on her hip, looked at the barn, and shook her head as though she couldn't understand it. Then she went on and gathered the gang in a huddle. They talked a minute and then marched across the road. I climbed out the window the way I had come.

While I was waiting for Midge, I located the spot where the wire came out of the barn. It went from the knothole to a tree and from that tree to another one. Then it curved toward the Sebastians'. If we had been looking, we probably could have seen the wire in several places from the playground. Naturally we hadn't been looking up in the trees for wires. Whoever had strung the wire had done a good job. The wire was high enough so it wouldn't ordinarily be noticed. Johnny must have used a ladder or climbed a lot of trees.

Almost five minutes went by and then Midge appeared. Behind her, strung out in a line, were all five of our little kids. They were looking very serious and walking very carefully.

"What did you bring the whole mob for?" I whispered. "We'll stand a fat chance of sneaking up on anybody with all them along!"

"Mom disappeared someplace," Midge said. "I had to

bring them. I've warned them all they have to be as quiet as Indians."

I didn't think much of our expedition's chances at this point, but we started off. We followed the wire without much trouble, but I can't say we were exactly noiseless in doing it.

The wire led toward the Sebastians' hedge, but about two-thirds of the way there, we came to the end of it in a big oak. About fifteen feet from the ground we could see a phone jack. It was exactly like the one on the speaker of Uncle Al's hi-fi set. You plug it into a connection on an amplifier. There was no sign of Johnny Sebastian, of any amplifier, or of a microphone.

"From up there he could see everyone," I pointed out.

"I guess he heard us and vamoosed," Midge said. "And it's a good thing because I'd scalp him if I caught him." She waved the hatchet in the air and did a silent war dance.

"I don't think he left in a big hurry," I said. "For this thing to work he has to have power. He must have strung three or four long extension cords out here from his house or garage. I imagine he just laid those along the ground. Even so, he had to coil them up and take them away. I think he saw you leaving with everyone and decided the fun was over for the afternoon. He gathered up his equipment and went home."

"Well, he'll have to gather up the pieces of his speaker

168

with a dustpan and put them together like a jigsaw puzzle because I'm going to chop it to bits!" Midge threatened.

"He may still be putting things away at his house," I said. "Let's go see."

We set off again in single file for the Sebastians' hedge. Midge and I knew the ground well because we used to chase the Apples' cat back through the hedge when the Apples lived there. We arrived at the hedge and peeked through into the Sebastians' back yard. There were three or four lawn chairs, and a hammock stretched between the trees. Dick Mayhew was lolling back in one of the chairs and somebody was in the hammock. On the grass beside the hammock was a microphone, several good-sized coils of wire, an amplifier, and a short section of ladder.

"That's Johnny in the hammock," Midge said.

"I wish we had had binoculars," Johnny's voice said. "It would have been fun to see the expressions on those kids' faces when they scooted out of that barn."

Dick Mayhew said something that I didn't catch.

"I wouldn't expect that little Glass midget to figure it out, but I thought Henry might. I guess he's not so sharp either."

Midge pressed her lips together the way she does when she's furious. There was a hole in the hedge a few feet away, and before I had a chance to say anything, she pushed through it. The five kids all followed her. I had to

wait until last or else jump over the hedge. I'm not that good a high jumper.

They saw us when we were about fifteen feet way. Dick Mayhew looked worried, but Johnny Sebastian began laughing like a lunatic. He sat up for a minute, looked at the expression on Midge's face, and then lay back in the

hammock, laughing so hard that the tears came to his eyes.

"Funny, eh?" Midge said. "Scaring little kids, you brave genius!"

"I think I'll send a little news item to the paper and radio," Johnny said, gasping for breath. "Henry Reed's Baby-Sitting Service keeps terrified kids in haunted barn."

He slapped his thigh and went off into another roar of laughter. His hammock was stretched between two sizable maple trees. The foot was attached to a big iron hook that someone had put in the tree, but the head rope was wound around the other tree several times and tied.

"You're a real cutup, aren't you?" Midge said. "Well, I'll just cut you down to size."

With that she swung the hatchet against the tree trunk, cutting the rope neatly in two. Johnny dropped like a ton of lead to the ground. He gave a painful grunt and stopped laughing. Midge had really sunk the hatchet into the tree, and I had to pull it out. We turned around and left without another word.

We had cookies and ginger ale in the barn. I don't think we'll have any more trouble with ghosts.

Sunday, August 22nd

Well, we've had another week of booming business. With the exception of Thursday, we've had at least three children every day. It's great being a successful business-man, but it can get sort of boring. I mentioned that to Uncle Al but he didn't give me much sympathy.

"Remember what I told you a month or so ago about ninety percent of anything being boring after a while? Now if you were at sea on a sailing ship, you'd spend day after day looking at the same ocean."

"That might be better than taking care of the same children day after day," I said.

"You might have a point there," Uncle Al admitted. "You don't have any statistics on how many of your former school teachers gave up teaching for the sea, do you?"

I don't think any of my teachers ever went to sea, and I don't know why my Uncle Al wanted to know. At any rate it was sort of a relief when Mrs. Caribelli asked me to come to her place yesterday. We had only one other job for two hours and Midge took care of that.

I didn't know who Mrs. Caribelli was when she called. Then she explained that she was the woman who owned the peacock.

"I don't want you to take care of any children," she explained. "Just a few animals. My mother, who lives with me, fell and hurt her leg and is quite lame. She can take care of herself, but I'd like someone here as I expect to be away for five or six hours."

"Just a few animals" turned out to be quite an assortment. There was a Nubian milk goat and a kid, five sheep with lambs, one ram that butted, a horse, the peacock, half a dozen Chinese geese, some Muscovy ducks, bantams of all sorts and sizes, some rabbits, and a pet raccoon. I think that covers everything that was outside. Inside she had two hamsters in a cage, a basset hound and a Siamese cat, four parakeets, and a macaw. She had all the animals listed on a pad and, opposite them, what they ate and how often. Feeding them all is such a job that I don't know when she finds time to cook dinner for herself and her mother.

Mrs. Caribelli's mother is a Mrs. Foulke. There isn't any Mr. Caribelli and I got the impression that he has been dead for several years. Mrs. Caribelli mentioned that her husband had built most of the outbuildings and the cages, so I guess he must have liked animals too. He would have been out of place there if he hadn't.

"I let Peppy out a good part of the day," Mrs. Caribelli said, stopping by the raccoon's cage. "He's lots of fun and will climb up on your shoulder. If you take him in the house, don't take him past the kitchen. He gets into too much mischief."

It was about ten o'clock when I arrived and it took us twenty minutes to tour the outside menagerie. When we had finished Mrs. Caribelli looked at her watch. "I have to go or I'll be late. I'll take you inside and introduce you to Mother. She'll tell you about things inside."

The introduction was brief. Mrs. Caribelli said in a loud voice, "Mother, this is Henry Reed. Henry, this is my mother, Mrs. Foulke. Henry is going to spend the day here and will feed the animals. Tell him what needs to be done inside. I've got to run."

Mrs. Foulke wore a hearing aid, but either it didn't work well or she kept it turned very low.

"What did you say your name was?" she asked after her daughter had gone. "Henry Peavey?"

"Henry Reed," I said loudly.

"Oh, Reeves. Are you one of the Baltimore Reeves?"

I decided to let the name go. "No, my father came from Michigan."

Mrs. Foulke was a rather heavy woman. She normally used a cane and because of her fall was unusually lame. It was painful for her to walk at all, so she spent most of the day in the living room. A good part of the time she was complaining about the TV programs.

"Nice quiet spot here in the woods," she said to me. "Very peaceful. There's nothing like a quiet peaceful day in the country."

"Mrs. Caribelli said you'd tell me what needs to be done here in the house," I said.

"Nothing needs to be done!" she said sharply.

"I mean for the animals."

"The thing that needs to be done to these animals is to chop off their heads," Mrs. Foulke said. "Those hamsters are silly little beasts. I don't know why Nell keeps them. The parakeets just eat all day, flutter their wings, and make a mess. That macaw is a loud-mouthed lunatic, and as for that stupid basset hound—a burglar could steal his tail and all he would do about it is cry. Abraham is the only worthwhile one of the lot."

"Who is Abraham?" I asked.

"That's Abraham," she said, pointing with her stick at the Siamese cat.

Abraham jumped on top of the TV set and looked down at the screen.

"It's time for his program," Mrs. Foulke said. "Turn on the set, will you? Channel four."

"You mean he watches TV?" I asked.

"Of course," Mrs. Foulke said. "Why shouldn't he? He likes cartoons best."

I turned on the TV and tuned in the program she wanted. Apparently she didn't intend to tell me what to do for the animals. I decided I could figure it out for myself and got up to leave.

"Nothing ever happens around here so you'll have to find something to amuse yourself," Mrs. Foulke said. "Come back and watch TV if you get bored, or read if you prefer."

I knew I couldn't stand the TV for long. I had it on quite loud but she wanted it louder. I turned the volume up until it practically blasted me out of the place and then went outside.

I had started toward the poultry house when I saw the horse eating on the front lawn. Mrs. Caribelli had warned me that he could open the gate if there wasn't a chain on it as well as the latch. The horse was wearing a halter, so I walked slowly toward him. I couldn't remember whether his name was Hector or Hannibal because I had heard so many names I was confused. When I got near he put his ears back and wheeled around so that his rear end was toward me. I tried circling, but he kept turning. He was a fat old horse and a greedy one. Even while he was maneuvering he kept eating. Five minutes later we had circled our way part way down the lane. I knew if we kept on in the same direction, he would eventually be out on the road and then I would have serious trouble. I was standing beside the lane trying to think of some way to get my hands on his halter when something hit me in the back and knocked me face down in the weeds.

When I got over my surprise, I turned over and there was the ram about to make another charge. He had been in the same pasture as the horse. I rolled out of the way and ran for the edge of the woods with him after me. Mrs. Caribelli had said that he was playful, but I didn't like that kind of play. I found a heavy stick and started toward him. He put his head down and charged. I bopped him on the nose, which seemed to startle him. I kept swinging the stick and he kept backing up. Finally I backed him into the pasture and closed the gate. The horse had wandered back in the front yard and was standing in one of the flower beds, but I decided to wash the dirt off my face before I went after him again.

I was drying my face at the sink when Mrs. Foulke shouted my name.

"Would you be kind enough to change the program?" she asked. "Abraham doesn't like it."

The cat was still on top of the television with his head over the edge looking down at the picture tube.

"Do you think he can see anything that way?" I asked. "Everything must be upside down."

"With most of the programs today it doesn't make much difference," she said. "They make just as much sense upside down. What have you been doing?"

"Chasing the horse," I shouted.

"Oh, Hector. Take a couple of sugar cubes and whistle. He'll come running."

She was right, and three minutes later I was leading him back to the pasture. I had scarcely put him where he belonged when I heard some frantic baaing from the next pasture where the ewes and lambs were kept. I went over to investigate.

Most of the lambs were almost as large as their mothers. One of the largest had stuck his head in a plastic bucket. Somehow the wire handle had flipped over his neck and there he was with a bright red plastic bucket over his head like a muzzle. He was scared silly and running around in circles trying to shake the bucket off.

First I tried chasing him. I went around and around the pasture but I couldn't catch him. Twice I almost had him trapped in a corner but the other sheep got in the way. Sheep like to stick together in a flock, and half the time they aren't running anyplace in particular but just to join other sheep. The trouble was I couldn't keep up with any of them and after three or four laps I was winded.

I decided the only thing was to drive them all into the barn. I had to chase them out of the pasture they were in and through a second one. Finally I got them all in the barn and locked the door. They milled around like a bunch of lunatics. I got near the one with the bucket on his head and made a dive for him. It was a real struggle.

We rolled over on the barn floor and he kicked me in the stomach, but I held on. I got him down on his side and sat on him. I was reaching for the bucket when it fell off. I got up, brushed off my clothes, and let the sheep out. Naturally they didn't want to go back to their original pasture and I had to chase them some more to get them there.

When I finally finished with the sheep I went back to the house. On the way I opened the door to the raccoon's pen. Peppy didn't seem too friendly. He looked at me suspiciously and went to the far corner of his pen. I left the door open and went back to the house to see if Mrs. Foulke needed anything. She and Abraham were still watching television.

"Oh, it's you again," she said when she saw me. "You're sort of wandering around like a lost soul, aren't you? I told Nell there was no need for you to spend the day here. There's not enough to keep an active boy like you busy. Why don't you take a little ride on Hector?"

"I think I'll have lunch first," I said. I was still puffing from chasing the sheep.

I went out to the kitchen and got out the sandwiches Mrs. Caribelli had made. She'd told me to fix up a tray with some cottage cheese, a pot of tea, and a sandwich for Mrs. Foulke. I put my own sandwich and a glass of milk on the tray and went in the living room. We had lunch in front of the TV set. For someone who said the programs were all terrible, she seemed to spend quite a bit of time watching them.

"Watch Abraham," she said proudly. "He won't look at the commercials."

A commercial came on and, sure enough, Abraham got up and wandered around the room as though stretching

181

his legs. As soon as it was over he went back to his spot on top of the TV.

"That's the strangest thing I've ever seen," I said.

"Nothing strange about it at all," Mrs. Foulke said. "He's not interested in deodorants, detergents, or cigarettes. He's not going to buy anything."

I took the tray to the kitchen and put the dishes in the dishwasher. I was about to go outside to look at the Chinese geese and the peacock when I heard a knock at the kitchen door. When I answered it I found two cub scouts in uniform. Their bicycles were parked a few feet away. A large cardboard box had been fastened to the rear luggage carrier of each bike.

"We're delivering the light bulbs Mrs. Caribelli ordered last week," one scout explained. They had the order carefully written down. She had ordered six one-hundred-watt bulbs, six seventy-fives, some sixties, and some forties.

"There aren't any seventy-five-watt bulbs here," one scout said, looking through the pile of bulbs on the step.

"I got lots on my bike," the second boy said.

He went back to his bike and brought another big box of light bulbs. They counted out the right number of each size and told me what Mrs. Caribelli owed them. I went inside to Mrs. Foulke and managed to explain the situation. She had me get her purse and gave me the money.

When I got back to the door I found the two boys playing with Peppy, the raccoon. He had decided to be friendly and they were having a wonderful time letting him climb up their clothes and sit on their shoulders. As I opened the door to hand the nearest scout the money, Peppy gave a leap through the open door into the kitchen.

"Here's your money," I said. "I've got to go. He's not supposed to go into the rest of the house."

Raccoons have odd black rings around their eyes which give them a funny curious expression. I watched Peppy amble around the kitchen with his back arched, the way raccoons walk. Suddenly he leaped on the kitchen table. I had forgotten to put away the container of cottage cheese. I beat him by about an inch. I picked up the container and he began climbing up my arm. He perched on my shoulder and stayed there while I walked to the refrigerator.

I wasn't thinking. He had already gone through one door in a flash, and he had tried to grab the cottage cheese before me. In spite of this I was dumb enough to open the refrigerator door with him on my shoulder. I leaned over to put the cottage cheese on a lower shelf and that was all he needed. He jumped from my shoulder to the second shelf and grabbed a cheesecake.

There was a wild battle. He grabbed the edge of the aluminum pan with his rear paws and one front paw. With the other paw he began scooping out cheesecake and stuffing it into his mouth. It was a soft, creamy cake and what he did to it and to me and to the kitchen is difficult to describe. We were all a mess. When I finally got the pan away from him, that was about all I got. The cheesecake had been splattered everywhere.

I put Peppy outside and began to clean up the kitchen. There was a pile of old newspapers in a closet and I wiped up the big globs with newspaper. Then I washed off the refrigerator, the front of the sink, and the table with a sponge. Finally I located a mop and mopped the floor. The wastepaper basket, which had been half full to start with, was now overflowing with messy newspapers. I decided to take it outside and empty it.

"I'm going outside for a few minutes," I said to Mrs. Foulke from the door of the living room.

"Good idea," she said. "A boy shouldn't be moping around in a house on a day like this. Get some exercise."

I found some matches and started outside with the wastepaper basket. On the steps were two packages of light bulbs that the cub scouts had left. Since Mrs. Caribelli's were inside, they must have forgotten these. Somebody was going to be short on their order, but I didn't know how to get in touch with either of the scouts.

Behind a little building that Mrs. Caribelli called the woodshed, I located a steel drum that was used as an incinerator. I dumped the paper in it and after wasting about three matches, got it lighted. Some of the papers were damp from my cleanup job, and there was quite a column of smoke. Although the incinerator was off by itself and seemed safe enough, I decided I should wait a few minutes and make certain. I'd had enough trouble.

I was watching the fire when the peacock appeared from around the corner of the poultry house and started toward me. It was the first time I had seen him the entire day. He was strutting very slowly, spreading his tail in a fan as he came. He was beautiful and I stood quietly so I wouldn't alarm him. After the adventure Craig and I had had when we were camping, I looked in the encyclopedia and read what there was about peafowl. The encyclopedia agreed with Mrs. Caribelli that the peacock does most of his screaming in the early morning or at dusk just before he goes to roost. However, like a rooster that crows early in the morning, he can crow any time. Abernathy strutted back and forth a few times and suddenly let out his horrible scream of HELP! HELP! Even though I was halfway prepared for it, I jumped about two feet. It's odd that such a beautiful bird should have such an ugly voice.

My jump must have upset him because he yelled "Help" once more and then moved off. I stood watching the fire for another five minutes and then started toward the house. I was about halfway there when a fire engine came tearing through the woods. It braked to a stop in the clearing and two men jumped off. On one side of the engine it said "Cherry Hill Volunteer Fire Company."

"Where's the fire?" one asked.

"There's no fire," I said. "I was burning the trash, but otherwise there hasn't been any fire."

"We got a call from a boy who said there was a fire and that someone was yelling for help."

"There's a crazy peacock that lets out a yell that sounds like *help*," I explained. "But no one here called in any fire alarm."

"False alarm," the man said finally, a trifle disappointed.

The driver hadn't turned off the motor. He began backing and turning to swing the big rig around. The third time he backed up, he went too far and the rear step hit the yard water faucet beside the garage. Something broke and water began to spurt out all over the edge of the driveway.

I waved my arms and pointed. The man who had asked me about the fire jumped off and looked. After the first spurts, the water wasn't running so fast but still it was flooding the whole area.

"Hey, Mac, we snapped off a yard faucet!"

The driver got down from the fire engine and looked. He said something that I didn't catch and started for the garage.

"Where's Mrs. Caribelli?" he asked as he got near me.

"She's away. I'm in charge."

186

"Then come with me. I'm going to shut off the pump. You come along so you'll know what I'm doing. I helped install this, so at least I know where the pump is."

I followed him to a small cinder-block building that backed up against the garage. It was actually part of the garage but had a separate door. Inside he lifted a trap door in the floor. Down below was a pit with a pump and a pressure tank.

"Just one main line leaving the tank!" he said in disgust. "That outdoor faucet must come off the main line that goes to the house. There's no way I can turn it off without turning off everything." He reached up and threw a switch. "Well, you now have no water pressure."

"We'll send a plumber," he said on his way back to the fire engine. "Tell Mrs. Caribelli I'm sorry. You might get a shovel and start digging where that faucet was. It's all got to be dug up before it can be fixed."

The fire engine left. I found a shovel and started digging. I had a hole about two feet deep when Mr. Wildblood arrived.

"Hear you had a little accident," he said cheerfully. "Well, the fire company is footing the bill, although I suppose it will end up with my donating my labor."

Mr. Wildblood and I dug the hole much bigger and a lot deeper. Then I handed him tools while he installed a new valve. It was one of those valves that you turn off be-

187

neath the ground so that it won't freeze in the winter. The fire truck had not only snapped off the pipe but had cracked the valve.

It was almost five o'clock before he was finished and we had filled the hole. Mr. Wildblood left and I raked the area smooth again. After that I fed the poultry. I was really tired by the time I went back in the house. On my way I noticed that the package of light bulbs was gone. I supposed the cub scouts had come back for them, seen my fire, and heard the peacock screaming. Like good scouts they had helped by telephoning the fire department.

Mrs. Foulke was reading. I sat down in another chair and picked up a magazine.

"Did I hear someone come in earlier?" she asked, looking up from her book.

"The fire department," I said.

"I suppose they were on their annual fund-raising drive," she said. "Nell always gives them something. They'll have to come back when she's here."

She went back to her book and I went back to my magazine. A few minutes later Mrs. Caribelli came home.

"Well, how's everything been?" she asked.

"Quiet, very quiet," Mrs. Foulke said. "Nice, peaceful day."

I was too tired to give Mrs. Caribelli the whole story, so I simply said that the fire truck had come by mistake and

188

had broken the faucet and Mr. Wildblood had repaired it. I forgot about the cheesecake and she probably thinks I ate it. I'm glad today is Sunday. Sunday is supposed to be a day of rest and I need exactly that.

Sunday, August 29th

The summer is about over and we are closing the Henry
Reed Baby-Sitting Service. Midge and I have made quite
a bit of money.

We're going to take the next few days off. We want to go
to New York City for at least one day and Uncle Al has
promised to take us. My father and mother will arrive in
Washington, D.C., in about a week and naturally I will
join them.

We had another week of good business. Belinda didn't
disappear, no one heard any spooky noises in the barn,
and I haven't had to chase any animals. Altogether it has
been a quiet week. Yesterday was more exciting, but you
can't really say we were baby-sitting. The Henry Reed
Baby-Sitting Service donated its day to charity.

Each year the Suburban Woman's Club puts on a fund-raising drive and gives the money to a scholarship fund for local high-school graduates. They've had all sorts of events—tours of old houses, dinner dances, and theater shows. This year they decided to have a sort of country fair with an antique show and auction. Most of the women of Grover's Corner belong to the club and it was decided to hold the fair in the field next to the McMurtys' house. It's a nice level five-acre pasture and ideal for the fair.

Mrs. Glass was on the fair committee and so was Mrs. McMurty. Aunt Mabel belongs to the club as well as three or four other women here in the Corner. For the past three weeks, all anyone has talked about has been the Country Fair. And for the past week you've never seen such a bustle of activity.

They had all sorts of attractions at the fair. They sold hamburgers, hot dogs, soft drinks, and desserts like ice cream, cake, and pie. There were exhibits by various organizations such as the Cherry Valley Rescue Squad and the Boy Scouts. There were the antique show, a baby contest, a dog show, and a big sale called the White Elephant Sale. I guess that and the Great Hay Ride operated by the Henry Reed Baby-Sitting Service were the two outstanding events of the fair.

Uncle Al has a sizable wagon that hooks on behind his garden tractor. Last year he had a two-wheeled cart, but he traded it in on this bigger four-wheel model. It's perfect for a hay ride. Midge and I worked for several days fixing it up for the fair. We washed and repainted it. We fastened posts at all four corners of the cart and rigged a striped awning to shade the passengers. Above the awning we fastened a piece of light plywood running the length of the cart. We painted this and I lettered a sign. The background of the sign was dark green and there was a daisy at each end. We painted both sides so that when the wagon went by, you saw the sign no matter where you stood. The sign said:

RIDES BY
HENRY REED'S BABY-SITTING SERVICE
HENRY REED AND MIDGE GLASS, OWNERS

The letters were bright red and really stood out. Although the summer is about over and I won't be doing any more baby-sitting, we might want to operate again next year. As Midge pointed out, it doesn't hurt to be well-known; we might want to run for political office some day.

We filled the bottom of the cart with pillows and charged ten cents a ride. We toured the fair and then went down the lane and made a short tour of Mr. Baine's farmyard. He has cows, chickens, and pigs, so that part of the trip was very popular. We could crowd as many as eight small kids in the cart. Uncle Al donated the gas for the tractor so all we collected went to the scholarship fund. Midge and I were donating our time.

We took turns driving the tractor. We were busy more or less steadily from the time the fair opened at eleven in the morning until about midafternoon. Of course each of us had time to eat and enjoy the fair while the other one was driving. Shortly after three there was a lull. I was waiting for more customers when Midge appeared, all excited.

"You'll have to postpone any more rides for a few minutes. We've won an award and we have to go get our medal or whatever it is."

I didn't know what she was talking about and thought she was trying to pull some sort of joke. She wasn't, however. Mr. Adams' radio station had sponsored the baby show and the dog show. Along with the prizes for these two shows, they gave an award to the best exhibit and a special award to the Henry Reed Baby-Sitting Service.

A platform had been erected near the center of the fair. It was used by the auctioneer in selling all the white-elephant items. The sale had started at one-thirty, and at three the auctioneer announced a recess of twenty minutes. It was at this time that the radio station announced the winners.

Midge and I had seats on the front row for the ceremony. First they announced the winner of the baby contest. It was a little girl about six months old and she cried the whole time Mr. Adams was talking. Next they gave a prize to a French poodle. It ran between Mr. Adams' legs

and almost tripped him with its leash. Besides it wasn't half as fine a dog as Agony. I'd entered Agony in the contest, but he hadn't won anything. Of course the judges might have known that Midge and I were winning another award and not have wanted to give too much to one person.

Next they awarded a prize to the Girl Scouts for their

exhibit. They saved us until last. Mr. Adams made quite a speech: "As you all know we honor a local business each month. We award what we call a certificate of merit to that business which in the station's opinion has most contributed to the community."

Midge nudged me at that point and I missed a sentence or two. In fact most everybody did. There was a slight commotion. Craig Adams was standing very near the edge of the platform. I hadn't seen him before, so I suppose he had just arrived. He had been trying to attract my attention and finally Midge had noticed. When I looked down at him he held up a little box.

"I got a garter snake," he said proudly.

The day we went on our hike we had tried to catch a garter snake but hadn't been fast enough. I had explained that garter snakes were not only harmless but actually a big help around a garden. I like snakes, except the poisonous kind, and I felt very pleased that I had convinced Craig not to be a silly 'scairdy-cat about them. I clasped my hands together and held them up to show that I thought he'd really done something.

Craig spoke in a loud, high-pitched voice and Mr. Adams looked down and frowned. Craig wasn't paying any attention, however. He grinned at me and asked, "Want to see it?"

I didn't have time to answer. He took the lid off the little white box and the snake slithered out. What a ruckus

196

there was! You would have thought a scorpion was loose! Finally Craig caught the snake again and all the hubbub stopped.

"That young man who just released the snake was my son," Mr. Adams said. "My apologies. It's a harmless garter snake but not exactly an addition to the occasion. As I was saying, we honor that business that we feel best exemplifies the ideals of American enterprise and community service."

I missed another sentence or two at this point. From what Aunt Mabel said, it was the best part too. Mr. Adams told about how enterprising Midge and I had been; how we were such careful and efficient baby-sitters, and how resourceful we had been in emergencies.

The reason I missed most of this was that Danny Wittenberg took advantage of our being up on the platform and unhooked the wagon from the tractor. He gave it a push and jumped in. The tractor had been parked on a slight upgrade and the ground sloped toward the road. The cart started rolling backward. He had no way of steering it or stopping it and it was headed straight for the road. Knowing Danny, I knew he wouldn't worry about a thing. He'd plan to knock any cars out of the way. I didn't want to interrupt Mr. Adams, but somebody had to do something.

"Hey! Somebody stop that cart!" I yelled, getting to my feet and pointing.

Two men were talking near a parked car by the road. One heard me and ran after the wagon. By this time it had veered and would have missed the driveway and have gone into the ditch. That wouldn't have done either the wagon or Danny any good. The man grabbed the side and managed to stop the cart just in time.

"I'm sorry to interrupt you, Mr. Adams," I said.

"That's quite all right," Mr. Adams said. "This merely illustrates what I was saying about Henry Reed's Baby-Sitting Service. It's always on its toes."

Just at that point I saw Mrs. Osborn up on her toes and trying to look over the crowd. She looked worried and annoyed. I knew right away what was wrong.

"Belinda's disappeared," I whispered to Midge.

"I know," Midge said with a giggle. "And I don't need a crystal ball to find her. I saw her hide. She's in that big trash barrel over there, and she's wearing a white dress."

"And so we take great pride in awarding this certificate to the Henry Reed Baby-Sitting Service as the Business of the Month," Mr. Adams announced. He produced a framed certificate and turned toward us. We were both supposed to walk over to the microphone, accept the award, and say a few words. Midge was trying to signal to Mrs. Osborn where Belinda was hiding and she missed the cue. I had to yank her by the arm to make her wake up. We walked over to the center of the platform and shook hands with Mr. Adams.

THIS IS TO CERTIFY
THAT THE
HENRY REED
BABY-SITTING SERVICE
HAS BEEN AWARDED THE TITLE OF
BUSINESS OF THE
MONTH

"Won't you say a few words?" Mr. Adams asked.

I'm not very good at making speeches. "I just want to say that both Midge and I are very proud of being picked as the Business of the Month," I said. "We want to thank all our customers for the business they've given us. Baby-sitting has been hectic at times, but we've enjoyed it."

"Thank you, Henry. And you, Miss Glass."

Midge stepped up to the microphone.

"I really haven't anything to say except to second Henry's words," she said. "It's an honor to be an outstanding business. I might take this opportunity to tell Mrs. Osborn that Belinda is hiding in that trash barrel over by the cake stand."

Midge took the certificate and I started back for the tractor and wagon. Mrs. Glass and Mrs. Ainsworth came hurrying up to me.

"Henry, Mrs. Ainsworth told me some time ago that she would donate a Victorian sofa for our White Elephant Sale and I forgot all about it," Mrs. Glass said. "Do you suppose you could go get it with the tractor and wagon?"

"I'll try," I said. "Will it fit in the cart?"

"I think so," Mrs. Ainsworth said. "Mr. Ainsworth is at home. He'll show you where it is and help you load it."

There was a length of heavy rope lying nearby that had been brought to rope off the parking area but hadn't been used. I tossed it in the cart in case I needed it to tie the sofa. I told Midge where I was going and drove off.

The White Elephant Sale was a sale of all sorts of things that people donated. Uncle Al claimed that it was mainly junk and he and Aunt Mabel got in quite an argument about it.

"Everyone cleans out his basement and attic and gives all the stuff to the sale," Uncle Al insisted. "Then all the women go buy all the contents of one another's attic. All they do is exchange cast-off junk and claim they got rare bargains."

Getting the sofa wasn't much of a job, however. It was in a shed in back of the Ainsworths' house and all we had to do was carry it out through the door. It fitted in the wagon without any trouble and I didn't bother tying it.

As I turned out of the driveway onto the road I saw the Sebastians' red MG parked beside the road about fifty feet ahead of me. Johnny Sebastian was beside the car looking under the hood. He was stalled. I grinned, stuck my nose in the air, and gave the tractor more gas. I was sailing by the MG when Johnny hailed me.

"Hey, Henry. Give me a hand, will you?" he asked.

"What's the trouble?" I asked, coming to a stop.

"I don't know. It just conked out. I'd like to get it home without having to pay for a tow truck. Dad may be able to fix it when he gets home. He's good with cars."

I knew that he was hinting for a tow. The tractor could pull it easily enough. In fact Johnny could move that little bug all by himself, but he couldn't push and steer at the same time. We were at the opposite end of Grover's Corner from the fair. The Sebastians were just a short distance beyond the fair on the other side of the road. The distance wasn't much, a tenth of a mile at most.

"You don't suppose you could deliver that and come back and give me a tow, do you?" Johnny asked.

"I can give you a tow right now," I said, remembering the rope in the wagon.

"That might be too much for that little tractor," Johnny said. "I can wait."

I knew he wasn't worried about the tractor, but about how he would look being towed behind the wagon with the sofa.

"There are lots of customers waiting for rides," I said. "I haven't got time for two trips."

He didn't like it but we tied the rope to the rear axle of the wagon and to his MG. The tractor had plenty of power and in a few minutes we were rolling along at a good clip. Midge had gone to her house for something and she came out as we approached. She took one look and dashed back in the house. I looked back a minute later and saw her come out with her camera. I had planned to take Johnny home and then double back to the fair with the sofa. When I saw Midge with her camera, I changed my mind. I didn't say a word, but when I came to the driveway to the fair, I took a quick turn and gave the tractor more gas.

"Hey, where are you going?" Johnny asked.

"I've decided to deliver the sofa first," I shouted over

my shoulder. I had to make a big circle to get to the auction stand. By the time I arrived Midge was there in front
of me, snapping pictures as though film were free. I
stopped, shut off the engine, and held up my hand.

Half the people at the fair had turned to see what was
happening because that little tractor isn't exactly quiet.

"Yes, young man?" the auctioneer asked.

"Henry Reed's Baby-Sitting Service is delivering an-
tiques for the auction," I announced. "Just the sofa is for
sale. The car is conked out and I'm giving it a tow."

Johnny was burning. Two men lifted the sofa out of the
wagon. I started the tractor again. I drove on out of the
pasture and this time I took Johnny and his car home.
There wasn't much he could do except thank me, which
he did sort of grumpily.

I drove back to the fair and found Midge.

"Wonderful finish to our business career!" she said. "A
stroke of combined genius and dumb luck! Wait until you
see the story and the picture."

"What story and what picture?"

"Mr. Sylvester was here. He got two or three pictures
too. And I gave him a few miscellaneous scraps of information."

"What kind of information?"

"Things like Johnny Sebastian's name and the fact that
he and Ruth are always bragging about that MG and how
fast it is. Mr. Sylvester doesn't have to be hit on the head

to get an idea. Do you know what he's going to say beneath the picture?"

"What?"

"Henry Reed's Baby-Sitting Service and John Sebastian's car in a photo finish."

Mr. Sylvester is a good newspaper man and can think of some snappy headlines. I'd call the fair a big success and the Great Hay Ride a big success. All in all, I'd say the whole summer had been successful. As Midge said, pulling Johnny Sebastian's red MG into the fair was the final touch. I'll be gone when the paper comes out, but Midge will send me a copy.

I've saved some money from my baby-sitting and I guess I've learned something. Uncle Al says I've probably learned a lot more than I realize. I still think I'd rather be a sea captain, only for different reasons now. It's quiet and peaceful out at sea.

About the Author

KEITH ROBERTSON was born in Iowa and grew up on farms and in small towns throughout the Midwest. His family moved a great deal, and at one time or another they lived in Kansas, Oklahoma, Minnesota, Wisconsin, and Missouri.

Mr. Robertson writes: "During the Depression, much of my career was dictated by a fanatical aversion to washing dishes. The only job I could find to finance college involved washing dishes, so I joined the Navy instead. When I discovered that midshipmen at the United States Naval Academy did *not* wash dishes but were gentlemen by act of Congress, I promptly applied for entrance. I succeeded and graduated with a B.S. degree."

When World War II began, Keith Robertson went into the Naval Reserve and then to sea on a destroyer. He is still in the Reserve and holds the rank of Captain.

The author, his wife, son, and daughter now live in central New Jersey on a small farm. This location, not far from Princeton, is the model for the general area in which Henry Reed's adventures take place.

Some of the true-life misadventures of Mr. Robertson's "baby-sitting" daughter inspired in part *Henry Reed's Baby-Sitting Service*.

The MS READ-a-thon needs young readers!

Boys and girls between 6 and 14 can join the MS READ-a-thon and help find a cure for Multiple Sclerosis by reading books. And they get two rewards — the enjoyment of reading, and the great feeling that comes from helping others.

Parents and educators: For complete information call your local MS chapter, or call toll-free (800) 243-6000. Or mail the coupon below.

Kids can help, too!

- - - - - - - - - - - - - - - - - - - -

Mail to:
National Multiple Sclerosis Society
205 East 42nd Street
New York, N.Y. 10017
I would like more information about the MS READ-a-thon and how it can work in my area.

MS Mystery Sleuth

Name_____
(please print)
Address_____

City_____State_____Zip_____

Organization_____

MS-10/77

A PUBLIC SERVICE MESSAGE FROM DELL PUBLISHING CO., INC.